'You don't h
something?'
thing like
Beginners. Or *Twins for the Terrified...*'

Rose smiled again. 'Yes, I have a book,' she agreed. 'Not that I figure on needing it. I tell you, my babies are not coming for three weeks!'

'But babies are certainly on their way,' Tom said, kneeling beside the great, mournful dog. 'By the feel of Yoghurt's belly, I'd say we definitely have pups coming.'

'What, now?'

'Watch out. The puppy's coming.'

For ten seconds, Tom's attention was taken with the puppy. And then he looked back.

Rose had sagged back to a sitting position on the floor. There were beads of sweat on her forehead and her eyes were wide with fear.

'No,' Tom said flatly. *She* was scared! *'No!'*

'They're coming,' she whispered. 'My babies are coming.'

Marion Lennox is a country girl, born on a south-east Australian dairy farm. She moved on—mostly because the cows just weren't interested in her stories! Married to a 'very special doctor', Marion also writes hugely popular stories for Medical Romances™. In her other life she cares for kids, cats, dogs, chooks and goldfish, she travels, she fights her rampant garden (she's losing) and her house dust (she's lost!)—oh, and she teaches statistics and computing to undergraduates at her local university.

Recent titles by the same author writing as Trisha David:

BRIDE 2000
MARRIAGE FOR MAGGIE

TOM BRADLEY'S BABIES

BY
MARION LENNOX

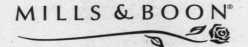
MILLS & BOON®

All the characters in this book have no existence outside the imagination of the author, and have no relation whatsoever to anyone bearing the same name or names. They are not even distantly inspired by any individual known or unknown to the author, and all the incidents are pure invention.

*First published in Great Britain 2000
Harlequin Mills & Boon Limited,
Eton House, 18-24 Paradise Road, Richmond, Surrey TW9 1SR*

© Marion Lennox 2000

ISBN 0 263 82086 6

*Set in Times Roman 10½ on 11½ pt.
02-0007-49995*

*Printed and bound in Spain
by Litografia Rosés, S.A., Barcelona*

CHAPTER ONE

IF SOMEONE had told Tom that by the end of the day he'd have delivered nine babies, he would have turned and headed for Darwin. As it was, he didn't even stop.

He couldn't. It was pouring—a vast river dumping from the sky. Sure, he should pull over and wait until it was safe, but he was on vacation. There was no emergency. He couldn't pull strings to delay his flight, and he'd had enough of this country.

But then there was the dog, right in front of the car.

He hauled frantically on the wheel. The car slewed sideways, skidding crazily in the water over the road—and the side of his sleek little sports car smashed squarely into the oncoming truck.

Rose was close to the end. All she wanted was her bed. Sure, she should pull over and wait for the storm to ease. Her ancient rattletrap of a truck wasn't safe in weather like this, but heaven knew when the rain would stop, and her back ached as if it were on fire.

The car came from nowhere.

She caught a glimpse of something…maybe a dog…right in the middle of the road, and then there was a car sliding sideways straight at her through the rain.

There was nowhere to go. She closed her eyes, shoved her foot hard on the brakes and waited for the crash.

'Are you okay?'

It was a female voice. Tom opened one eye and winced.

5

He opened the other eye and winced again.

There was rain bucketing through his smashed windscreen, and there was something past the rain...

It was a face, peering anxiously through the broken glass—and it was some face!

Gorgeous, he thought dazedly. Just gorgeous! The face had huge blue-grey eyes and freckles, but just the right amount. Her freckles were scattered over flawless skin and her soft, brown hair was plastered wetly in an elfin cut.

There weren't too many women who'd look gorgeous when they were as wet as this, he decided—in a muddled sort of way—and managed a lopsided grin in answer to her worried expression.

What was she asking? he thought stupidly. Was he okay? Somehow he made himself decide.

'Um...yes.'

'You're sure?' The voice was still desperately anxious.

The fog cleared a little. The pouring water had one good effect—it was definitely helping to clear his head. Now he looked out into the woman's eyes and really focused. As well as worry, there was exhaustion etched on her face, and the exhaustion was deep-grained, as though it had been there for ever.

'Your car's smashed,' she said, and her worried voice was lovely, to match her face.

Tom tried thinking this through, but thinking was hard. He must have been knocked stupid. He was aware that he was grinning like a Cheshire cat—and grinning was definitely stupid, because, yes, his car was smashed!

Tom's sleek little Alfa Romeo, hired for the short time he was in the country, was hardly built to withstand being rammed by a...

By a what? Somehow he managed to focus on what was through his smashed windscreen and past the woman's face—and there was a large Dodge truck halfway into his Alfa.

Good grief!

So... Was he in fact okay?

He gave one foot a tentative wiggle, and then the other. No pain! Maybe his feet had fallen off! Maybe that was why he couldn't feel them.

'Your car's smoking,' the voice said helpfully. 'Maybe we should get you out.'

That'd be good. Tom thought about smoking cars for about two seconds flat, and suddenly found himself agreeing entirely. The fog cleared like magic. If there was one thing Tom knew about it was fires, and sitting in smoking sports cars didn't make a good disaster plan at any time. But...

'I don't think you can get out of your door,' the woman told him. 'It looks like it's buckled into my truck. You'll have to pull yourself out the other side. Hang on...'

Five seconds after that, while Tom was still hauling his miraculously intact feet from the mangled remains of brake and accelerator, her face appeared at the passenger window. Blessedly, the passenger door swung open at her touch.

Anything would, Tom thought, in his semi-dazed and slightly stupid state. Anything would open for a woman like this!

'Can you slide across to this door?' she said. 'You're not stuck?'

'No.'

But, in fact, sliding was easier said than done. He was too big to slide across two tiny bucket seats. He was six foot two and powerfully built...

'Can I help?' She started to lean forward, but then there was a sharp intake of breath and the face withdrew from sight. 'I'm sorry,' she said faintly, from somewhere out in the rain. 'I don't…think I can bend. I—I'll get a fire extinguisher from the truck.'

There was another gasp, and suddenly Tom was hauling himself backwards out of the car as if it were already on fire.

Up until now he'd been concerned about himself, but in the woman's voice he was hearing pain. Bad pain. Forget me, he decided fast. He was suddenly dead worried about her.

Two minutes and a heap of physical contortions later he had managed to wriggle his body free and haul himself out into the rain.

The face was gone.

He must have been dreaming, he thought in confusion, staring around as the rain dumped down on top of him. He'd imagined her being just by the car—maybe even collapsed on the road—but she was gone. His head was starting to thump. Maybe he'd imagined her.

No. Sure, he'd had a bump on the head, but he'd definitely seen her. Tom stood and stared about him through the driving rain, and tried to make himself think, while the heavens tipped rivers onto his head.

Apart from the crashed vehicles, there was nothing. This was a deserted country road—or maybe it wasn't usually deserted but the locals had too much sense to be out now. There were paddocks around him, and a couple of soggy Hereford cattle hanging their heads over the fence in idle interest…and there was nothing else.

Or maybe there was something beyond the ten yards it was possible to see, Tom thought, as the cold water started clearing his head, but any more than ten yards distant was hidden by rain.

The face must be somewhere. Maybe over the embankment…

'Is anyone here? I can't see.' Tom took three or four

steps forward—and staggered. He'd hit something, and it wasn't a woman.

The dog was standing wetly, square in the centre of the road. At thigh height, Tom hadn't seen her, but he did now. He couldn't miss her—and he didn't. He came crashing down right over the top of her in an ungainly sprawl, to end on his knees on the gravel.

This, then, was the cause of the crash. Somehow Tom bit back an oath—the owner of the face might still be in earshot—and staggered to his feet while he stared down at the huge bloodhound bitch. The dog was standing motionless, pathetic and resigned. Waiting to drown in the rain...

Had he hit her?

The more he looked, the more it seemed he hadn't. The dog showed no signs of external injury, though Tom didn't think he'd ever seen such a heap of canine misery in all his life. She stood in desolate, quivering solitude, all saggy jowls and vast mournful eyes. She was so thin that her ribcage was almost piercing her hide, but her belly was distended with pregnancy.

One starving, sodden bloodhound, swollen with pup...

Tom's gut wrenched in sympathy. What a sight! He knelt and cupped his hands around her face in a futile gesture of comfort—but that was the best he could do. Short of an armload of towels, a good feed and a warm fire, there was nothing he could do now to help her.

'Hey, girl, it's okay. I didn't hit you,' he told her. 'We'll sort you out in a tick. But, first, where's the lady?'

The dog looked at him mournfully, but she didn't move. It was as if it was beyond her to shift an inch.

Tom could spend no more time with her. He rose. Priorities... The lady... The voice... The pain.

She must be someplace.

'Is anyone here?'

He felt stupid, calling out into the rain to nothing. Someone must be here. The rain was blinding!

'Where on earth are you?' She *must* be here.

'I...I'm here.'

The face emerged from the rear of the truck, and the face was attached to a woman holding a fire extinguisher. The extinguisher was almost as big as she was. As Tom watched, the woman took two staggering steps toward him—and crumpled.

He caught her before she hit the ground. One thing Tom Bradley was good at was moving fast in emergencies—that was what his job was, after all! Now was no exception. His arms swept her up easily and, as he lifted her body against him, he had his next surprise. The lady was as pregnant as the bloodhound.

Maybe more so. Her waistline was vast. The rest of her was slight almost to the point where she matched the bloodhound in the malnutrition stakes, but there was no mistaking her pregnancy under the sodden shift she wore. She gasped as he lifted her, a gasp so low he almost didn't hear it. She was definitely in pain...

But she was already recovering.

'I—I'm sorry. Please...put me down. I'm okay.'

'You'll fall if I do.'

'I won't. I must have tripped or something.' She was getting her strength back, and her voice steadied. 'The fire extinguisher's heavy.'

'Yeah, right,' Tom said morosely. 'You can't carry the fire extinguisher because it's heavy. Well, I'm carrying the fire extinguisher and I'm carrying you—plus whoever else you have on board—and it doesn't bother me at all. Are you hurt?'

'No. Honest.' She gave an emphatic wriggle to try and make him lower her—and her waistline moved. It definitely moved! Tom eyed her bulge the way he'd eye a rattlesnake poised to strike.

Uh-oh... This was right outside his ken. He might be trained to cope with emergencies, but pregnant ladies weren't in his job description.

'You sure you're not hurt?' he managed, still staring in fascination at the bulge. 'You sound as if you're hurting.'

'I'm not hurting.' She fixed him with a look of sheer determination, her lovely blue-grey eyes luminescent with rain. 'Honest. I'm fine. I climbed out of my truck all by myself, which is more than you did. Stop staring at the twins and put me down. Please?'

Twins... Good grief! But there was no way he was putting her down. 'No, ma'am,' he said apologetically. 'Not until I find you some place dry.'

'The truck, then.'

'The truck?'

'In case you hadn't noticed, it's hardly damaged,' she said with asperity. Her strength was flooding back, and indignation with it. 'No thanks to you. Do you always drive like a madman in conditions like these?'

'There was a dog.'

'A dog...'

'In the middle of the road. I didn't want to hit it.'

'So you hit me instead.'

'I'm sorry, but...'

'My driving instructor told me never to swerve to avoid an animal,' she said sternly, and, amazingly, there was suddenly a twinkle in those gorgeous eyes. 'She said you're even more likely to hit it if you swerve, because they don't know where to dodge. But then—' she sighed '—my driving instructor was female. She's from the sensible half of the species! The half that aren't soft where animals are concerned.'

'You don't say,' Tom growled back, and it was impossible to suppress a smile. She twinkled up at him again in the rain, and he stared down at her in fascination. Drowned and battered and…laughing?

'I certainly do.' But then her laughter died. Her eyes clouded again, and her sparkle of mischief faded. She didn't groan, but he could see a groan was there, held back with superhuman effort. The pain was back with a vengeance.

'You are hurt,' he said in concern.

'No. I just—I just have a backache. I had it before we crashed. Because of the twins.'

'The twins?'

'You've already been staring at them,' she said carefully, lifting her hand as a shield so rain water wasn't running straight down her freckled nose. 'You have noticed that I'm extremely pregnant?'

'I did notice that,' Tom said, just as carefully. 'You do look a bit in the family way. Twins, eh…' He took a deep breath—he was way out of his depth and afraid he might go under any minute. He didn't want to ask his next question, but somehow he must. 'You're not…you're not in labour, are you?'

'No.' That was definite, anyway. 'No way. They're not due for three weeks, and my doctor says they shouldn't come early.'

'No?' Tom had started moving again, carrying her easily around to the passenger side of her truck. 'You're huge. You look like you'll deliver any minute to me.'

'Are you a doctor?'

'No, ma'am.'

'Well, there you go, then,' she said firmly. 'So I'll thank you kindly not to cast nasturtiums at my waistline and we'll agree to follow doctor's orders here. If he says these twins are staying where they are for three more weeks, then that's where they're staying.'

'You plan on having obedient kids?'

'You bet. What are you doing?' He was striding around the truck, carrying her effortlessly.

'Putting you in the truck.'

'But…' She gave a futile wriggle. He gripped her harder and she gave up until he deposited her tenderly in the truck. Then she stared out through her windscreen, which was miraculously intact. 'This isn't much use.'

'Why not?'

'I might be dry, but we're not going anywhere. Some dope's parked a sports car right where I want to drive.'

That made him grin. 'They should do something about the parking in these parts,' he agreed mildly. 'You'd think they'd have provided more than two parking spaces in the last hundred miles.'

'And I was here first,' she told him darkly.

'Sorry, ma'am.' His grin deepened. This was some lady! 'I'll try to do better next time. My driving instructor obviously failed me in parking, too.'

'You know, I think we want a tow-truck,' she said reflectively, staring out at his smashed car.

He nodded. 'We agree on that, but let's just clear this smoke first.' He had his head clear enough now to plan. 'You keep still and look after your twins. Tell them it's raining outside and they should stay inside and play.'

'But…'

'No arguments.' His head hurt and there was still the threat of fire. He took the fire extinguisher from her hands and left her to twin control. 'Stay!'

And he left her.

First things first, and the priority had to be one smoking engine. If the Alfa caught fire, then the truck would burn too.

With a fire extinguisher—especially the mammoth extinguisher the lady had produced—the thing was no problem. He hauled the wheel jack from the Alfa's tiny trunk and used it to jemmy up the smashed bonnet of the Alfa. Thirty seconds later, the engine was a mass of foam, and there was no way any fire stood a chance.

He'd hardly needed the extinguisher, Tom thought bleakly, drinking rain water. Once the engine was exposed to the elements, any fire would have been drowned at the first spark. This rain was crazy.

What now?

What he wanted most, he decided—before a tow-truck— was an ambulance. The woman might say her babies weren't coming for three weeks, but there was real pain in her eyes and he wanted her checked.

But how to call an ambulance? Or even a tow-truck?

This was one of the few times in his life Tom wasn't carrying his mobile phone. Apart from one hold-all, he'd left all his gear at the airport. Tom spent his life on the end of his phone, and for this month of enforced rest he'd made sure it was silent.

But he wanted it now. The thought of his phone being a hundred miles away was enough to make his gut twist in dismay.

There wasn't a house in sight—in fact, thinking back, he couldn't remember seeing a farmhouse for miles. This land was undulating cattle country, a land of vast holdings with houses few and far between.

So how far were they from the nearest town?

He ducked his head into the smashed Alfa and retrieved his map—emerged again, changed his mind and ducked back into the shelter of the car to read it. Reading maps in this weather was like trying to read pulp.

He was dripping so much water that the map almost was pulp anyway by the time he had it figured, and even then it didn't help. He'd left Kingston half an hour ago and passed nothing. According to the map it was half an hour on to Weatherby, and neither town looked big enough to have what he needed—a hospital, a decent emergency department and an obstetrician.

There was a whimper at his leg and he looked down.

The dog. Oh, heck, the dog... Add her to his list, he told himself. She needed a vet. So he needed an ambulance, tow-truck and vet... Where were they all?

Uncontactable. There was only Tom.

'Hey, I'm sorry, girl. I almost forgot you.' He stooped and lifted the pathetic pooch into his arms and she didn't offer any resistance. There was no greeting whimper or wag of her tail. Nothing. The dog lay limply in his arms, as if she was past caring.

Here, then, was another responsibility! His mind racing, Tom walked back through the rain, pulled open the driver's side of the truck and placed the dog inside.

'Here you go. Have some company,' he told the woman. 'This lady looks like she might have backache, too.'

The woman stared across at her new companion. 'Good grief! Is this the...?'

'The cause of the accident,' Tom said morosely. 'Yep. And pregnant? You bet. I hope her pups are as well behaved as your twins. So talk among yourselves. Discuss bootee patterns or something. Just don't have any babies—either of you—while I try to figure this mess out. You don't have a phone, do you?'

'Not here—mobile phones don't work out here anyway—but there's one at my house.' The girl was staring down at the dog in concern. 'Oh, no... She looks exhausted. She looks starving!'

'How far's your house?'

'About a mile on.' But she was hardly listening. She fondled the dog's big ears, and the bloodhound put a weary head down on her knee and closed her eyes. Two pregnant ladies finding comfort in each other's presence.

'A mile?' Tom prodded helpfully.

'I guess. It's no more than that. When this rain eases we can walk.'

'We can't walk. Not if you want to keep those twins on board.'

The girl thought about that for a minute and appeared to accept it. Which made Tom more uneasy. Just how bad was her backache? 'Then what will we do?' she asked.

The dog opened her eyes again and swivelled her big head to look up at him. So did the girl. They looked at him, lady and dog—wide blue-grey eyes and huge brown ones—and there was an expression on their faces that Tom recognised. Trust! He'd figure something out.

'Okay, okay, I'm figuring,' he said hastily, and closed the door on the pair of them. 'Just give me a minute.'

Sure he'd figure it out.

Or maybe not. Give him a good raging inferno any day, he thought bitterly. Real drama—the sort a man could sink his teeth into. Not this. He liked his emergencies uncomplicated.

If the rain would just clear. He couldn't see.

He shoved the wet hair out of his eyes. Damn, he should have had a haircut when he was in Rockford—the black curls were unruly enough even when they were dry. He took himself around to the front of the truck. It was wedged hard into his car, and the car's engine was pulverised. The Alfa was a write-off.

But maybe the Dodge could be salvaged.

He bent down and checked the truck tyres and engine mounting, and what he saw cheered him enormously. While the dog and the girl stared out at him through the windscreen, he started jemmying bits of Alfa away from the truck. If he could clear it…

He did. Ten minutes later, the buckle of interlocking metal had been untwisted enough to let him see the damage. They'd built their trucks to last thirty years ago! The truck was almost intact. Even its radiator was okay. There were scratches and buckles, and the right front tyre was ripped from the wheel—but maybe it was driveable.

Driving with a flat tyre would be hard on the wheel rim, but it was damaged anyway—too damaged to let him put the spare tyre on—and letting it chop into the road surface was definitely the lesser of two evils. If the girl's home was only a mile off...

What choice did he have? Damage the truck a bit more? Damage the road a bit? Or deliver babies himself? What sort of choice was that? He wanted help, he wanted it now, and there was a telephone a mile away. With no rubber on the tyre it'd be a bumpy trip, and that might be a disaster— but maybe...

They'd just have to cross their legs and hold on, he decided definitely. No babies!

So five minutes later, with a very pregnant bloodhound draped across his legs and with a very pregnant lady by his side, Tom persuaded one ancient engine back into life and bumped the truck carefully southwards.

Her home was a farm, set way back from the road. It was beautiful, in a soggy kind of way. Once the sun came out, it could be gorgeous. The willows along the drive were weeping their hardest, the driveway was awash and, as they pulled up by the front porch, the sound of the rain pounding on the roof was almost deafening. There were roses planted all along the front of the house and the smell of their wet blooms was wonderful.

'This is my home,' the lady said as they pulled to a halt by the front door, and Tom gave her a sharp glance. Apart from curt directions, she'd hardly spoken, and now her face was pinched and pale. 'You...you want to come inside?' she asked.

Now *there* was an offer! Seeing the alternative was to sit in her truck indefinitely, the thing looked pretty certain, but Tom looked at her pinched face again and he hesitated at what he saw. Was it...fear?

'Hey, I'm not a villain,' he said quickly. 'It's safe to ask me in. Is there someone else at home? Your husband?'

'I don't think you're a villain.' she said wearily. 'Maybe I don't care anyway. There's not a lot to steal, and I'm way past being ravished.' She flashed an attempt at a smile at him and Tom blinked. She really was extraordinarily lovely—and there was raw courage on her face. He could see she was still in pain, yet she was pushing it away just as hard as she could. 'And no, there's no one else here,' she went on. She hesitated and then put out her hand. 'Maybe it's time we introduced ourselves. I'm Rose. Rose Allen.'

Tom took her hand in his and found it warm and strong. He met her smile and felt his gut give an unexpected twist. This was some lady, he thought again.

'I'm Tom Bradley.'

'And who do you think this is?' she asked, and put her hand down on the dog's soft head. The bloodhound was three-quarters asleep, her vast body still draped across Tom's knee and her flanks gently steaming.

There was a battered leather collar around the dog's neck, no registration tag but a plastic name disc, and the disc looked suprisingly new. Tom lifted it while the dog slept on.

'According to this, her name's Yoghurt.' he read.

'Yoghurt,' Rose said blankly. 'A bloodhound called Yoghurt! I don't believe it. Do you suppose that's what she eats?'

'I don't think Yoghurt eats anything much at all,' Tom said. 'She looks starving.'

'Well—' Rose managed a smile and shoved open the

truck door '—let's find her some food, then. Let's find us all something to eat and warm us up. Welcome to my home.'

The farmhouse was huge. Tom followed her up the wide steps and into the hall—slightly hindered by his armload of dog. He'd offered to leave the dog on the porch but had been met by a look that told him he was stupid to suggest such a thing.

'This is a farmhouse,' she'd said simply. 'We're used to dogs.'

We... And...*dogs*?

The plural didn't make sense. *We* might be used to dogs, but there was no 'we' here, and there were no dogs. There was nothing and nobody to meet them.

Rose led the way down the central passage, her hand resting on the small of her back as she went so he knew she was still hurting. The place smelled musty and unused. There were rooms off to each side—maybe ten rooms or more before they reached the back quarters—but they looked closed for the duration.

'I'm sorry. It's a long hike through the house. Normally I'd drive round to the rear but I didn't think the truck would make it,' she said. She pushed open a door and motioned for Tom to carry the dog through.

This, then, was where she lived. It was a vast kitchen-living room, its stone-flagged floor covered with ancient rugs. A vast cooking range had been left burning while she was away—it was warm enough now to heat the room to comfort levels. There was a Baltic pine table, and chairs big enough to feed an army, and there were faded old chairs and a settee built for comfort. And size.

It was a fabulous room, Tom thought, staring around at the jumble of shiny pots hanging from the ceiling, and at the wide windows at the end opening onto a grape covered pergola, with a view of the country stretching for miles and miles. In this room you'd be tempted to ignore the rest of the house. Which, considering what he'd seen of the rest of the house, might be just as well.

As Tom stared, Rose was stooping awkwardly to toss a couple of cushions from the settee to the floor in front of the cooking range.

'Put her down here,' she said, her voice soft in sympathy. 'Let's get her warm, poor girl.'

The dog looked up from Tom's arms to Rose, her mournful eyes agreeing with her entirely as Tom settled her on the cushions.

'Do you think her babies are due soon?' Rose asked. She lifted a towel that had been hanging by the stove and stooped over the dog, but Tom was before her. He took the towel from her hands and started rubbing.

'If her babies don't come soon, then she'll explode,' Tom said, towelling the big dog gently over her flanks. They were stretched to the limit. Given a town, given a phone, he'd call a vet.

Given a phone, he'd call a doctor. A doctor—and he was towelling a dog!

'Okay, first things first,' he said, rising.

'Yeah. Dry clothes, some dog food and a cup of tea for us. Unless you'd like a beer?'

A beer... he'd kill for a beer—but something told him it was the last thing he needed right now. He needed a clear head, and it was fuzzy enough as it was. He needed the phone.

'We'll get you some help first. Your back... The pain...'

'It's eased,' Rose said, but there was something about her voice that told Tom she was willing it to ease rather than believing it had.

'Get yourself settled on the sofa,' he said. 'Point me to

the phone and tell me where I can find you another towel and something dry for you to put on.'

'I can get it.'

'You heard.' He lowered his voice to a growl. 'Sit yourself down and put your feet up. And point me to the phone.'

'I don't need to...' She reached for the kettle, but Tom was before her, lifting it from her grasp and carrying it over to the sink brooking no argument.

'I'll pick you up and put you on the sofa if you don't go of your own accord,' he told her. 'Let's play this safe. No babies. At least until you have help. Sit!'

She cast an uncertain glance at him—and he glowered right back at her. Then she really looked at him. His face was brown, rugged, strongly lined and determined, and it told her he meant exactly what he said. He was a man accustomed to giving orders, and there weren't many who'd argue with Tom Bradley in organisational mode.

A girl knew when she was beaten, Rose decided, and in truth she was glad to lose this argument. Her legs hurt. And her back...

'Yes, sir.' She sat.

'Phone?'

She pointed a finger at the far wall and Tom crossed to it with urgency. He was looking at her face...

'Who are you calling?'

'An ambulance.'

'I don't want an ambulance.'

'Remind me to ask next time I want to be told what you need,' he growled. 'I need an ambulance even if you don't, and the reason I need it is because I'm worried. You, lady, have had a bad jolt, and those twins of yours have had a bad jolt too.' His brow snapped down as a sudden appalling thought hit. 'You don't suppose... I mean, I've heard that seat belts can hurt in pregnancy...'

She'd obviously thought this through way before he had.

'If my babies are in foetal distress then they have a pretty funny way of showing it,' she said bluntly. 'But thanks for trying to scare them to death anyway. They appear to be kicking their mother in indignation. Want to feel?'

Tom stared—then backed away as if he'd been burned.

'Hell, no.'

She grinned. 'Coward.'

'Yep. Absolutely.' He turned resolutely back to the phone.

'You're not ringing an ambulance.'

'You still need to be checked.'

'I won't…'

But she paused at the look on his face. He'd lifted the receiver and was listening, holding the receiver away from his ear, listening again—and then giving the receiver a thump on the cradle.

He tried again.

Nothing. His face said he heard nothing.

'It's dead.' He stared down at the phone as if it had betrayed him.

'Rats,' she said, far more cheerfully than she really felt. In truth, a medical check wouldn't be all that unwelcome. 'It'll be the storm. Now you can't call the ambulance.'

'No, and I can't call a mechanic either to fix the car. Or a vet. You realise we're stuck? It was as much as that truck could do to get us here. There's no way it'll get us into town.'

'No, but…' Rose's smile faded. She stirred uneasily, and unconsciously her hand went to the small of her back again. 'It's no matter… Surely… I mean, it'll ease soon. The line will be fixed…'

'Where's your family? Your husband?'

Her face closed. 'I don't have…family.'

Oh, great. No one! Surely she didn't live in this barn of a place alone?

So think laterally, he told himself, pushing away the sudden, inexplicable desire to ask more closely about her husband. Now wasn't the time. 'How close is your nearest neighbour?' he demanded.

'The closest farm's derelict,' she said. 'Absentee landlord. There'll be no phone there. It's been allowed to run wild for years. To the north is National Park and there's no one. The next occupied farm is six miles away—and even if we made it there they're on the same phone line as mine. If our phone's dead, theirs will be too.'

She had to be kidding!

'You haven't thought,' Tom said carefully, 'that it might be a trifle unwise to live six miles from the nearest help when you have twins on the way?'

That got to her. 'I'm not stupid,' she snapped. 'I've organised to rent a room in town. I'm going in next week to stay until they come.'

'Gee, that helps a lot now.'

'They're not coming now.'

'No.' He took a deep breath and tried calming down. No. Maybe they weren't. Please... But...

'You don't have a good handbook or something?' he said. 'You know, something in the style of *Brain Surgery for Beginners. Twins for the Terrified.*'

That made her smile again. 'Yes, I have a book,' she agreed. 'Not that I figure on needing it. I tell you, they're not coming!'

'But babies are certainly on their way.' he said morosely. He filled the kettle and put it on the stove, then crossed to kneel beside the great, mournful dog. 'By the feel of Yoghurt's belly, I'd say we definitely have pups coming.'

'What, now?'

'She's not moving,' Tom said. 'Dogs get anxious before

their pups are born—restless—trying to find a decent spot.
By the feel of the muscle spasms she's having, that time's
past. That's probably why she was standing in the middle
of the road and didn't move even after I almost hit her.
She's had her restless time and found nowhere safe and
dry. Until now. At a guess, I'd say this is her first litter.
She looks like there's things going on with her body that
she doesn't understand.'

As if on cue, a rippling spasm caught the great dog and
her body shuddered. Tom held her face in his hands and
looked deep into those sad eyes.

'Hey, girl. It's okay. You're okay.'

'How do you know all this?' Rose asked from the sofa.

'There was a dog—when I was a kid.' Tom's voice was
suddenly clipped, and his tone told her that any more questions wouldn't be welcome. She stared—and then stared
harder as Tom's weathered face softened into a smile. 'Hey,
I think we might have one on its way right now,' he said.

'A pup?'

'I certainly hope it's a pup. If it's a kitten we have a
problem. Where's your book?'

'My book talks about breathing and support roles and
not panicking,' Rose said breathlessly. 'Not what to do if
a puppy turns out to be a kitten. Let's read it later. For
now, I'm watching.' Tom looked up sharply as she came
and knelt on the floor beside him.

'I told you to stay on the sofa.'

'And miss the birth? No way.'

'You'll have your own babies soon enough. Sooner if
you don't do as you're told.'

'I told you. Three weeks.'

'Rose…'

'Watch out. The puppy's coming.'

It was, too. Yoghurt gave an awful heave, and a grunt
of absolute exhaustion. Then another heave—and the first

of the puppies slid out onto one of Rose's gorgeous cushions.

'She's ruining your cushions,' Tom said softly, in truth not even thinking about the cushion but mesmerised by the puppy and concentrating on sliding the membrane clear from its tiny wrinkled nose. Normally the bitch would do this herself, but not Yoghurt. There were more pups coming, she was past exhaustion and if she managed to get all her pups out it'd be a miracle.

'My cushion will have died in great and valiant service,' Rose breathed—like Tom, her eyes not leaving the tiny wet nose. 'Isn't he just beautiful? I can imagine no higher honour for a cush...'

She stopped, mid-word. Another puppy slid out.

For ten seconds, Tom's attention was taken with clearing the next little airway. And then he looked back.

Rose had sagged back to a sitting position on the floor. Her hands were flat on the rug behind her, and her fingers were white with pressure. There were beads of sweat on her forehead and her eyes were wide with fear.

'Oh, no...' she whispered

'No,' Tom said flatly. *She* was scared! *'No!'*

'I—I'm afraid...' Her voice faded and that indomitable courage slipped. She reached out in a gesture of entreaty and he caught her hands and held them.

She held him back, gripping his hands as if she were drowning.

'They're coming,' she whispered. 'My babies are coming.'

CHAPTER TWO

DOMESTICITY was not Tom Bradley's strong point.

Neither were babies.

Family life for Tom had been a succession of his mother's disastrous relationships. He had no brothers or sisters—he'd been a mistake himself, and there was no way his mother would risk another. The dog he'd told Rose about had belonged to yet another of his 'stepfathers', and by the time the pups were weaned he and his mother had been long gone.

All through his childhood, Tom had watched his mother try marriage over and over. She usually chose nice guys, who often cared for the kid who tagged along at her side, but he'd learned the hard way not to grow attached. As soon as he could, he'd taken himself far away from his mother's relationships—and any relationships, for that matter. He kept as far from emotional ties as he could get.

Plus anything else that went with emotional ties. Like housework, cooking, mortgages...

And babies!

So he'd seen puppies born, but he'd never seen a human baby born—and he didn't want to start now! Tom sat on the floor and gripped Rose's hands—and panicked like anything!

Somewhere he'd seen a notice: 'When all else fails panic!' That was what he felt like now. He didn't need any notice telling him how. He was making a fine fist of it all by himself.

How far away had Rose said the neighbours were? Six miles? Yeah, great. They might just as well be two hundred.

The rim of the truck wheel had been cutting into the road all the way here. The edges of steel were now almost flat. With the extra rain, the steel rim would sink—they'd been darned lucky to make it here—and he'd be bogged. And Rose would be alone.

He couldn't leave her.

Nor could he walk six miles. Even if he ran, it'd be at least an hour before he was back here—providing he found someone.

So… You're all she's got, Tom, boy, he told himself fiercely, and the panic started all over again.

He was panicking!

Rose made it back to the sofa and took deep breath after deep breath, fighting to keep her panic at reasonable levels. Reasonable meaning she wasn't screaming blue murder.

She was alone with a bloodhound giving birth and a complete stranger…

Who on earth was he? She knew nothing about him.

One thing was for sure—he wasn't medical. Even if the panic in his eyes didn't give that away, his clothes sure did. He looked as if he lived outdoors—the strong, muscled country type. Blue jeans. Khaki, short-sleeved shirt with an open neck and a six-pack of a chest under it. Leather work boots and a face that was worn almost as leathery by harsh sunlight. His black curls were lighter at the tips, and his blue eyes were creased. From sunlight or laughter? Or both.

Was he a farmer? He'd coped with the puppies okay. Could he cope with babies?

Yes, her heart pleaded, but she looked at his face and saw panic there that matched her own. He'd helped her to the sofa, but now he was staring down at her as if she were an unexploded bomb!

Heaven help her…only heaven was a long way off, and if heaven couldn't help her…

Well, someone had to be calm, she told herself desperately. It looked as if it would have to be her.

So what was new? she thought bleakly. It was always Rose who coped. What on earth had made her think childbirth would be any different?

'I think,' she said unsteadily, 'that we need more towels.'

'Towels,' Tom said blankly. 'Yeah, right.'

'They're in the bathroom. Third door on the right. Oh, and hot water. Fill some pans and put them on the stove.'

'Why do we need hot water?'

She stared up at him.

'Don't you know?'

'No.'

'Neither do I,' she admitted helplessly. 'But they always boil water in the movies.'

Tom stared. And saw the need in her eyes. He had to pull himself together here. If there was one thing this lady didn't need, it was a gibbering, panic-stricken idiot.

'Okay,' he said hastily, 'I'll boil water. We can figure out what we need it for later. Where's the book?'

'Book?'

'Twins for the Terrified,' he said. 'I need a manual here.'

'On the bench. First shelf by the stove.'

He grabbed it as if he was grabbing a lifeline, and started flicking through the pages.

'Tom.'

'I'm speed-reading,' he told her. 'Talk among yourselves.'

'Tom!' Her voice changed and he hauled himself out of his panic to look at her.

'Yes?'

'Please…can you hold my hand while you read?' she said desperately. 'Please…'

What followed was the longest night of Tom Bradley's life. Nothing had prepared him for this. At some of the rig fires—nights where men had lost their lives—sometimes he'd thought those nights were endless. This one, though, dragged on and on, each minute dragging him inexorably towards the climax.

'We need to get you dry,' he told her when he realised that the babies weren't about to burst onto the stage in a rush.

Yes, she was in full labour, but her contractions were still a couple of minutes apart— 'And that means I have a little time,' she'd whispered between pains.

So he'd stripped off her wet shift and somehow both of them had blocked out the unseemly fact that a stranger—a male!—was towelling her dry and fetching a warm night-gown to slip over her head.

And that she was just lovely...

Pregnant, distressed, frightened—she might be all that, but Tom still thought she was one of the most beautiful women he'd ever met. Which made no sense at all.

It must have been the bump on the head, he figured. That, or a reaction to terror...

Between contractions and puppies he speed-read the book, but as far as he could see it was full of instructions to panic. Sure, they weren't labelled Panic Instructions as such, but they might just as well have been.

Home Birthing...

Not to be considered if there is no medical back-up available.

Not to be considered in the case of multiple pregnancy.

To be approached with extreme caution for first-time deliveries...

And as for practical help... As far as Tom could see, short of letting her grip his hands as if she were drowning each time a contraction hit, all he could do was make sure everything was scrupulously clean, and hope like crazy the delivery was normal.

The book seemed pretty sure it wouldn't be.

'Primigravida…twins…no medical help…' Gloom, defeat and despair stared up at him from every page. Finally he stuck a marker in the spot which told him what to do when the birth actually took place and decided to ignore the gloom.

So, sound confident.

'I read that in the olden days peasant women toiled in the fields until their time, then retired behind a snook, dropped their bundles, thought of a name for it and then kept right on toiling.' he told Rose, with a brightness that fooled no one. Least of all him.

'How olden?—and do we have a snook?' she asked cautiously, and he grinned. She was wonderful. 'Do we even know what a snook is?'

'How about behind the sofa?' he suggested. 'I bet a sofa's a fine substitute for a snook.'

'On the sofa might be more comfortable—' She winced. 'Comfort… I've forgotten what it feels like.'

'Maybe you should be in the bedroom.'

'No way. It's warm in here and you can't look after Yoghurt and me at the same time…'

That was the one thing that took the edge off their terror. The puppies kept right on coming. Between each contraction, Rose watched anxiously as Tom cleared each new little airway.

Five…six…seven little airways. Seven tiny black puppies, blind as moles and each with tiny black droopy bloodhound ears—fourteen ears.

At the end, when it seemed there were no more puppies to come, Tom heated a little milk and helped Yoghurt to drink. The exhausted dog drank as if her life depended on it and, for the first time since he'd lifted her from the road, she stirred herself. She turned her big velvety head up to him and ran her tongue over the back of his hand—then looked across at Rose...

Then she sighed, and slept, while her puppies squirmed in a wriggling heap around her.

'It's as if she's saying thank you,' Rose breathed, with tears in her eyes. 'Oh, Tom.'

And for the life of him Tom couldn't stop a glassy sheen misting his eyes as well. Damn, it must have been the bump to his head...

And then the next contraction hit Rose. Tom washed himself with so much soap, it could have killed every self-respecting bacterium within a hundred miles of the place. Then he moved back to take her hands again as the thing started in earnest.

'I can't—' As he reached her she moaned and clenched her knees together, and he helped her into a half-sitting position. 'Oh, Tom, I can't stop it. I have to push.'

Tom gulped and glanced down at the manual. Pushing...stage two...

'Right. I guess you have to push, then. The book says it's okay to push.'

'Gee, thanks.' She cast him a despairing glance. 'Check the phone again.'

No point. He'd been checking it every three minutes, and by the look on Rose's face he knew there was no time to do it again.

'They're coming,' she moaned. 'Tom, I'm not ready.'

'I am.' He made his voice as strong and sure as he could, and he gripped her hands as if he was totally in control. 'Hey, I've read everything I need. I've sterilised scissors.

I've put the towels near the stove. They're warm and ready...'

'Tom.'

'Yes?'

'Just shut up and hold on!' She gasped and gasped again as another contraction hit, and then another. There was hardly any time between them at all.

There was no time to think. No time even to panic...

And five minutes later tiny Jessie Allen was born, bursting into the world with a yell to match her mother's. Two minutes after that, Toby Allen joined her.

In the end, Tom blessed his book. If things were supposed to be complicated by the fact that it was Rose's first experience of childbirth and she was delivering twins, then they'd been lucky.

There were step-by-step graphic pictures—and in the end it had been easier to look at what was really happening than look at the pictures. There were a heap of pictures of cords around necks, but theirs—the twins'—cords were just where they were supposed to go. Tom tied them and snipped like a real professional, wrapping each baby in a warmed towel and snuggling them against Rose's breast...

Snook or no snook, they'd done the thing!

By the time he'd cleared up it was dawn. Tom walked outside to the porch steps and stared down the valley. This was the most beautiful country.

There were undulating pastures with huge spreading gums, Hereford cattle grazing in the misting rain, and far below them the river was winding its way towards the sea.

He grinned, the aching dread of the last few hours disappearing to nothing. If he hadn't been worried about disturbing the brood inside, he would have let out a victory whoop.

Tom Bradley had just delivered nine babies, and he felt fine!

And then they all slept. The whole lot of them. Tom came in and Rose was huddled under the duvet, a tiny baby crooked under each arm and all eyes were firmly closed. On the cushions by the stove, Yoghurt snoozed placidly, and the puppies slept as well.

He tried the phone again. It was still dead. He still wanted a doctor but now...it didn't seem urgent. Everything seemed as if it was just fine!

He'd rest just for a minute, he thought as he hauled more cushions onto the floor and let his long body sink.

Just for a minute...

It was the last thing he knew until midday.

'Tom.'

He was awake the moment she whispered his name, sitting up as if a shot had rung out. He stared wildly round and found her watching him.

She was different. Changed. She looked serene and contented, her lips curved into a tiny cat-got-the-cream smile.

'What's wrong?'

'Nothing.'

Okay. He relaxed, but it took him a minute longer to get his bearings, and when he did he had to check all his charges. The two babies were lying peacefully by their mother. Yoghurt was still sleeping—past the point of exhaustion, she was sleeping as if she was making up for years of deprivation. In contrast, her puppies were squirming their way firmly round her teats.

Five, six, seven...all were present and correct. His chest

expanded a notch or two and he felt broody as a mother hen. All his charges were fine.

'You look like you should be handing out cigars,' Rose told him, and grinned as his colour mounted.

'Yeah, well…'

'You should, too. You did a wonderful job.'

He had. He grinned too, and for the life of him he couldn't stop.

'Tom?'

'Mmm.'

'I hated to wake you, but I have a problem.'

'A problem?' His grin faded. A problem. Never mind, he thought. He could cope with problems. After what he had just done, everything else faded to insignificance, and if everyone was breathing and sleeping without trouble then problems couldn't be too urgent.

'I'll walk to the next farm to get help,' he told her. 'I was going to last night but…'

'I don't need the emergency services—' she smiled at the look of apprehension on his face '—it's just…I'm getting a bit wet.'

'Wet,' he said blankly.

'I need two nappies,' she said apologetically. 'I don't think babies are meant to be wrapped in towels and nothing else.'

Nappies… Good grief!

'And I wouldn't mind help to go to the bathroom…' Her voice faded.

His eyes flew to hers, and with a jolt he realised that she was appalled at having to ask for help. It went against the grain for this woman to ask for anything, he thought. All last night—she'd hardly made a noise, all through her labour, and he knew how much it must have hurt. Only right at the end had she yelled, just the once for each baby. And

this morning she had stayed quiet. He wondered how long
she'd been awake, lying in discomfort, waiting for him to
wake and help her.

He felt contrite and stupid—and she saw it.

'Hey, I've only just woken, and you've done so much
for me anyway.'

'No worries,' he said gruffly. 'Let me get you to the
bathroom—and then let's handle nappies. I hope you have
another instruction book, lady! Nappies! What next?'

In the end they figured it wasn't just nappies the twins
needed, it was a full-scale bath. The babies were sticky and
bloodied and...

'And generally disgusting,' Tom announced, unwrapping
tiny Jessie and hastily wrapping her again.

'They are not. They're gorgeous.'

'Yeah, and I bet Yoghurt thinks those blind little worms
are gorgeous too,' he said morosely. 'Okay, we'll have to
bathe them, and I bet you could use a wash too.' Then he
cheered up. 'Hey, maybe this is what all my boiling water's
for.'

What followed was a very silly half-hour. Rose showered, while Tom stood at the bathroom door and fretted in
case she fainted or haemorrhaged to death or something.
She didn't oblige, so he helped her back to the kitchen-
living room.

Then came the bathing of the babies.

She had a baby bath, bought specially. He bullied her
back onto the sofa, wrapped in a fresh duvet, and set the
baby bath up on the floor. Then he made a trip to the room
she'd prepared as a nursery, and returned to lay everything
out like a battle plan.

'Two towels. Warm. One bar of baby soap. One warm
bath. Two jogging suits...'

'They're not jogging suits.'

'That's what they look like to me.' Tom held a little yellow suit up for inspection. 'All-in-one jogging suit. Revolting yellow. Did you choose this colour?'

'It was cheap,' she said defensively.

'Mmm.' Tom held the suits up in disdain. 'I can see why. You aiming to train the kids as runners?'

'No.'

He softened. 'I guess they'll be farmers,' he said, and saw the smile fade from her face. 'You should have bought them moleskins and wellington boots. Hey, is something wrong?'

'Nothing's wrong,' she said shortly, and made herself smile again. 'You're missing something.'

'What am I missing?' he demanded. 'Everything's here.'

'Except one thing.'

She handed over baby number one before he could demur. 'Here. Don't drop her.'

As if he would—but he was sure scared he would. 'I thought you might…' he said.

'I would, but—' she gave a shamefaced grin '—the shower…it took it out of me.'

Of course. So once again there was no option.

Tom didn't lack courage, but it took real courage to unwrap tiny Jessie's towel and lift the slippery little baby in his big hands. As he lowered her into the bath, her eyes flew wide open—hey, they were the same gorgeous grey-blue as her mother's—and she stared up at him as if she couldn't believe such a sensation existed. Warm water…

'She likes it,' Tom said in awe, swishing her gently back and forth in the warm water, cradling her gently in his big hands. 'Hey, she likes it.'

'She does, too.' Rose leaned down from her sofa and gently soaped the tiny body. 'Oh, Tom, she's lovely.'

She certainly was, Tom thought. And so was her mother…

Enough of that!

Jessie was a dream to dry and dress. She lay back in her warmed towel and savoured the feeling of being rubbed, hardly moving while Tom followed Rose's instructions— he manoeuvered her little legs into a nappy and wriggled her tiny body into her jogging suit.

'There's nothing to this baby caper,' Tom said smugly. He wrapped her in a woolly blanket, and lifted her back into Rose's arms. Rose unbuttoned the neck of her night-gown and lowered her daughter to her breast. Jessie nuzzled close, her tiny pink lips found what they were searching for—and she started to feed.

Rose looked up at Tom and her eyes were full of tears. And Tom practically choked himself.

'How does she know how to do that?' he breathed. 'Isn't she the cleverest thing?'

'Yep...' Rose swallowed a sob. 'Yes...'

'Hey, Rose, don't cry.' For the life of him he couldn't stop himself putting a hand out to touch her face, to stop the tears sliding down her cheek. 'You're not to cry...'

'I don't cry...'

'I can see that.'

'It's just that I'm happy.'

'I can see that, too,' he said softly, and his gut kicked in hard. Good grief! This wasn't *him*. This new sensation. It had nothing to do with him. Tom was unemotional. Detached. He'd taken a lot of trouble to get that way.

And somewhere these babies had a father...

'I need to bathe Toby,' he said, and leaned over her to retrieve the next bundle. Mistake. Leaning over her, he breathed in a waft of pure feminine scent. Soap and sleepy baby and something lovely...

The something lovely was Rose.

In something like desperation, Tom grabbed Toby and started unwrapping. And that was the end of their peace.

Toby took personal affront at having his small person bathed. He clenched his tiny fists into balls, screwed up his face into a howl of outrage and let his displeasure be known to anyone within a two-mile radius.

Rose watched with a contented smile while the boys did battle. By the time he was finished, Tom was almost as wet as Toby had been, and both faces were flushed red. Tom handed the bundle of noise to his mother, Toby found what his sister had…and peace mercifully descended.

There was a series of squeaks from the other side of the room. Tom turned to find that Yoghurt had risen stiffly to her feet, and the puppies were whimpering their protest.

'I bet she needs to go outside,' Rose said apologetically, and Tom sighed. He needed a good sit-down after that job.

He needed a beer…

Instead, he took Yoghurt out to where the sunlight was starting to glisten into a rainbow on the horizon, and watched while she sniffed out her new world.

What would happen to her? he thought. Would Rose keep her?

Maybe. Rose looked a soft touch.

You'd need to be a soft touch to keep a dog like Yoghurt. If ever there was a bag of bones…

Maybe she was lost. Maybe he could take her to the pound and let them find her owner.

Yeah, and maybe they'd put her down.

The dog hauled herself back up the front steps and came and nuzzled a weary head against his leg. He found himself crouching to give her a hug, and her wet nose hit his face in a slobbering lick.

'There's no need to get attached here,' he said to her. 'Be nice to the lady. She's your meal ticket. As soon as I get her some help, I'm out of here.'

The dog looked up at him with world-weary eyes that said plans were made to be undone. Yeah, right…

'I am. I'm due to be in Hawaii right now. I have a vacation to catch up with.'

Right...

There was a rumbling deep down in the dog's belly and Tom grinned. 'Okay. Vacation second. Food first. You have a family to feed so let's see if we can get something into you first. Come to think of it, we all need a feed.'

Great idea! A much better idea than emotion.

This was his first knowledge of her real poverty. Rose was still totally occupied with her babies so he hit the refrigerator and cupboards in search of sustenance.

What he found shocked him.

There was pasta and a few basic sauce ingredients. There was a little long-life milk, but no meat, not even in the freezer. And nothing else.

Hey, she'd been coming back from town when his car had hit her. Tom took off out to the truck and found a couple of soggy grocery cartons. More pasta. Vegetables, but basic and cheap. More long-life milk...

This was not the stuff to give nutrients to two nursing mothers and nine babies, he figured. Much less Tom, who was frankly ravenous.

He went back, tried the phone again and sighed.

'What's wrong?' Rose looked up from her nursing and her brow creased at his frown. 'Still no line?'

'No.'

'I guess... If you need to leave urgently you could always walk the six miles to the neighbours. Maybe Joan would give you a lift into town. If you paid her...'

'Neighbourly type, eh?'

'Not very,' Rose said shortly. 'She doesn't approve of me.' She bit her lip. 'Maybe with reason.'

'Oh, yes?'

'I'm not very neighbourly myself. But if you want to leave…'

He did want to leave. This place was so domestic it was starting to close in on him, but there were so many unanswered questions.

'I need to get you to hospital first.'

'No.'

He stared. 'What do you mean, no?'

'I mean I'm not going to hospital,' she said softly, holding her sleeping twins close. She looked up at him, her eyes pleading with him to understand.

'Tom, I never would have chosen a home birth. With twins, and with them being my first babies, and no help—well, a home birth wasn't an option. But I don't have hospital insurance and there's no one to look after the farm. I'd organised someone to feed the cattle while I was in hospital, but I really can't afford it, so now that it's happened…'

'You can't stay here.'

'Of course I can stay here. This is my home.'

'Who's going to help you?'

'I can manage on my own.'

'Oh, yes. Bathing the babies…'

'I'm weak today,' she admitted, 'but by tomorrow…'

'Oh, yeah,' he jeered, 'you'll be back to the paddy fields, working dawn to dusk.

'I'll be careful.'

'Don't you have anyone who can help without being paid?' he demanded incredulously.

'No one,' she said, and her voice was so clipped that he knew further probing was useless.

He changed tack. 'Then you need to go to hospital,' he said gently. 'You need to be checked, and have a good rest, have someone look after you.'

She tilted her chin. 'And who's going to look after Yoghurt?'

He hardened his heart and refused to look at the dog. 'Yoghurt can go to the pound. She's a stray, Rose. Her puppies will get good homes.'

'She won't,' Rose said definitely. 'She's as battered as me.'

'You're battered?'

'I mean exhausted.'

'Rose…'

'I'm staying here.'

'Look, you need to be checked,' he said, exasperated. 'The babies… Aren't there tests you're supposed to do to see if they're healthy? And you? You can't tell me you're okay when we haven't even had a midwife look at you. I'm no midwife.' He shoved his thumbs in the belt-stays on his jeans and glared down at her, coming to a decision. 'Okay, here's my plan. You at least need to see a doctor. I insist. If you won't go to a doctor then I'll pick you up and carry you.'

'I'll see a doctor,' she agreed. 'But Dr Connor will come here.'

A house-call. That was something. Surely a doctor could make her see sense? 'When?' he demanded. 'Now? I'll walk over and get help.'

'There's no need. As soon as the phone's on I'll contact him.'

'*We* will.'

'I beg your pardon?'

'The word is *we*.'

'I don't know what you mean.'

'I may be an independent bachelor,' Tom said grimly, digging his fingers hard into the sides of his jeans now and setting his jaw. 'I may not know the least thing about babies, and I may be the world's most helpless male—but until we can get this Dr Connor here you're stuck with me.'

'You mean—you won't leave?' He wasn't imagining it. He looked down into her face, and there was a tiny lessening of the strain around her eyes. Relief?

She was scared stiff, he saw. Scared stiff of being left alone.

'I… You don't have to do that.'

'My car's squashed,' he said. 'Until I get that organised to be de-squashed or replaced, I have no way of getting out of here.' There was no need to tell her it was a hire car, he figured. It was fully insured. A simple phone call to town would bring him another one, and he could be on his way.

'That's true,' she said, relieved. 'And it was your fault you crashed.'

'Yoghurt's fault.'

'And you'll need someplace to stay until it's fixed.'

This was starting to sound long-term! 'Yes, well, speaking of Yoghurt…' Tom said hastily. 'Let's get the rest of this family fed, shall we, Rose? Starting with the most needful and then working down. I think that leaves me last.'

CHAPTER THREE

BY THE time everyone was fed it was almost dusk. Where had the day gone? Tom wondered, wandering out to the front porch. He still hadn't made the journey to contact the doctor. There simply hadn't been time. Should he go now?

Yoghurt was at his side, taking a break from the demands of motherhood to stand pressed closely against his leg as he gazed down the valley. The big dog had eaten her pasta as though she was starving, and now Tom looked down at her with doubt. She needed meat. Calling a dog like this Yoghurt...

'You're not meant to be a vegetarian, are you, girl?' he growled, and she rubbed herself against him. The look she gave him was one of absolute devotion, and Tom found his heart sinking. The last thing he wanted was devotion!

He should be taking her straight to the pound. He had to walk away from here.

Involuntarily his hand crept down to rub behind her ears and she flattened herself against him some more.

Hell!

'You sure can't come to Hawaii with me,' he said. 'I'm a globe-trotter, girl. A mother dog and seven puppies aren't my scene.'

She nuzzled his hand and gave a faint whimper, and he sighed. This was getting crazy.

'You wouldn't like Hawaii.'

Her tail waggled.

'I fight fires. They're hot and dusty and dangerous and they don't make asbestos suits to fit bloodhounds.'

Her tail waggled some more.

'No!'

If dogs could sigh, she sighed. Finally she left him, casting a regretful look back as she returned to motherhood, and he stood out on the porch feeling bad for another ten minutes. Good grief, what was he thinking of—wondering how he could take a bloodhound with him on his travels?

Ha!

When he went back into the living room, Rose was swinging her legs off the settee.

Why? The twins had just been fed again and were sleeping soundly—in side-by-side cots now that he'd brought in from the nursery. They didn't need her.

He focussed on Rose's face. Maybe she was going to the bathroom, but he didn't think so. Her face looked determined, as if she was steeling herself to do something she didn't want to.

'Going someplace?' he asked politely.

'I thought I might get dressed.'

'Mmm.' He nodded politely. 'Expecting visitors?'

'No, but…'

'But what?'

'I thought I might go to check on the cows,' she said diffidently. 'It—it's been raining. Sometimes they get stuck in the boggy ground around the dams.'

'And you're going to pull them out with your bare hands.'

'No.' She set her mouth into a look of grim determination. 'I usually take the truck and dig and pull…but if I can't…Well, obviously now I can't take the truck…and I can't pull…and I know I'm not fit enough to dig…'

'So what will you do?' Tom's voice softened at the look of resolve on her face.

'I'll take the rifle,' she said. 'If I can't save them, I'll not leave them there to die.'

'You don't think—' he spoke carefully, looking down at

her bare toes on the faded rug '—you don't think it might be more sensible to ask for help? From me, for instance?'

'You've done so much already.'

'I hit your truck. Maybe I jolted the babies into arriving. Maybe this whole mess is my fault.'

She took a deep breath. 'This whole mess is *my* fault, as well.' 'There's no need to take all the blame. But if—if you'd keep an eye on the babies while I go?'

'No, Rose,' he said softly, then crossed to her and swung her up into his arms in one easy movement. He held her there for a fraction of a moment—a fraction too long. He knew then that he'd be checking her cattle. He knew he'd be doing any damned thing she wanted. Slowly, reluctantly, he lowered her back onto the sofa, then ran his hand over her close-cropped curls.

'You stay where you are, Rose Allen,' he growled, his voice unnecessarily harsh. 'You mind nine babies. I was going to walk over to the neighbours' and find you a doctor, but if you think they're in danger—I'll check your dratted cattle.'

In the end it was a relief to take off, to stride away from the house, a trusty spade over his shoulder and with a job to do that didn't involve domesticity. The rain had eased to a faint mist over the valley. The sun was setting and the air was warm and still. This was good! He was a man with work ahead. Men's work...

Men's work? She'd be doing it if he wasn't, he thought, remembering the look of determination on her face. She was as stubborn as he was.

So where on earth were her people?

There were too many unanswered questions here—certainly too many questions for him to walk away now.

Then he found his first cow. This was why she'd been

worried. The closest dam to the house was a circle of water in a sea of mud. Around the back it seemed stable enough, but on the south side it was a trap for the unwary, and there were two unwary. They were young Hereford cows, stuck to the flanks in mud.

Left on their own, they'd struggle until they either sank sideways and drowned, or died of exhaustion. Tom looked at them for a long time, trying to figure out an easy way to free them. There wasn't one. Finally he hoisted his spade from his shoulder and sighed.

What followed were two hours of hard physical work. Without any sort of winch, there was nothing for it but to dig the cows free. That or Rose's rifle…

'Stupid things,' he told them, but they looked at him with their great bovine eyes, and the look they gave him was one of trust.

Hell, everyone depended on good old Tom, he told himself impatiently. Even the cows!

Finally they staggered free in the moonlight. He gave them a lecture on the stability of mud and on common sense, but the gaze they gave him on departing was just as stupid as ever.

Why should we worry? their look said. We have good old Tom to dig us out!

Bovine twits!

After that, he traipsed the whole farm, finding one other cow in trouble in the furthermost dam. By ten o'clock he was filthy and exhausted—he had blisters on blisters from digging—and he trudged back to the farm feeling like an early Christian martyr.

She was waiting for him.

Tom opened the door to the kitchen-living room and blinked.

He'd told her to rest, but she hadn't. The big room was pristine. The mess had been cleared, Yoghurt and her pup-

pies were lying on fresh cushions and the baby parapher-
nalia was neatly organised. The babies themselves were
sleeping peacefully in their separate cots, and something
really good was bubbling on the stove.

'Pasta sauce,' she told him as he sniffed appreciatively.
She said it fast, apologising before he said a word, and his
brow snapped down.

'Hey, don't sound sorry. It smells great. That's not the
smell of the bought stuff I gave you for lunch.'

'I grow fresh herbs.' She smiled, and Tom stared. She
was dressed now, simply, in jeans and an oversized man's
shirt. Her feet were still bare. Her face was scrubbed fresh,
free of make-up, and her eyes were huge in her still weary
face. She looked young and vulnerable and very, very
lovely.

'How old are you?' he asked suddenly, and she laughed.

'Twenty-six—going on forty.'

'Going on sixteen, I'd say,' he said, and she grimaced.

'I've had a bit too much life experience to be sixteen.
How are my cows?'

'Dry.'

'How many did you have to dig out?'

'Three.'

'Is that all?' She flashed a smile at him. 'What took you
so long?' Then, at the look on his face, she chuckled, a
lovely lilting laugh that had him staring again. 'I'm joking,'
she said hurriedly. 'Seriously, I think you're wonderful. I
can't tell you how wonderful. But off with you to the
shower. Dinner's waiting.'

'I don't—' He stared down at his clothes, realising for
the first time that he was a muddy mess. But his only
change of clothes was back in his smashed car.

'Here,' she said triumphantly, and motioned to a hold-
all beside her. *His* hold-all.

'How...?'

'The local constabulary,' she said, and smiled again. It had exactly the same effect on his insides as her chuckle. Weird. 'While you've been playing with my cows, I've been entertaining.'

'Well, I'll be damned.'

'Don't swear in front of the children, sir,' she said primly. 'Do you want to hear what happened or not?'

'Yes, ma'am.' There didn't seem much else to say.

'Someone reported your smashed car to the police. It's not completely blocking the road but it looks bad. The police sergeant checked it, then figured that whoever was in it must have walked for help—so he came here.'

'Did you ask him to send out the doctor?' Tom demanded, getting right to the point.

'He said he would. I told him it wasn't urgent.'

'You *what*?'

'It's not urgent,' she said serenely. 'You must see the twins and I are fine. He said he'd organise the doctor to come tomorrow. Oh, and he's arranged for your car to be towed into town to the repair place. He says the phone will be back on by morning so could you ring him and give him your particulars.'

'He wasn't worried about knowing who I am now?'

'I told him you were a friend,' Rose said, and her smile faltered a little. 'I...if I hadn't...he might have insisted...'

'That I leave. I can understand that.'

'You won't leave, though, will you?' Rose asked. 'I mean— I thought you'd stay tonight. You can get a lift back to town with the doctor tomorrow.' Her voice faltered again and Tom knew exactly what she was thinking. Her face was transparent.

'No, Rose,' Tom said softly, watching her face. 'I won't leave tonight, and I hardly see how I can leave tomorrow.'

'You can. I'll be fine.'

'Yeah. Right. And pigs can fly. And Yoghurt's really a vegetarian! Ha!'

She faded right after the spaghetti. She had concentrated fiercely on eating but the talking and laughter had drained right out of her. It had all been an act, Tom thought as he watched her lay down her fork in resignation—an act to show how independent and strong she was.

She might be independent, but strong...no way! She pushed back her chair and made to lift the plate from the table, but as she rose she staggered and was forced to hold onto the table for support.

She was as weak as one of Yoghurt's pups! Tom was with her in half a second flat, holding her against him, and then, as her knees crumpled, lifting her into his arms.

He was getting used to it. This was starting to feel...normal. And good?

'Bed,' he said.

'I can...'

'No,' he told her firmly. 'Admit it, Rose. You're not Superwoman. You can't.'

'I must. Tomorrow—'

'I'll still be here tomorrow,' he told her, acknowledging the fact that had been in his mind for hours. At some time while he was digging out the second cow the impossibility of her whole situation had slammed home to him.

Whoever she was, he couldn't leave her.

'You don't belong here. I don't even know who you are.'

'I'll give you any character references you like, and I'm on holiday,' he told her. 'That holiday might as well be here. After all—' he shrugged and lied through his teeth '—I have to wait somewhere until the car is fixed. It'll take weeks.'

'You can't stay here for weeks.'

'So organise someone else to come.'

'I don't... I haven't...'

'There's no one to help you?' He shook his head. 'I don't
have a clue why that should be, Rose Allen, but for the
moment I'm accepting it as the truth. But you're not alone.
You have me. And now you're going to bed.' And he
started carrying her towards the door.

'In here,' she said distressfully. 'I'm sleeping here
with…'

'With me?' He grinned. 'No. I don't know you *that* well,
lady. Last night you had the sofa and I had the floor. I've
checked the rest of the house. There's a perfectly comfortable bedroom across the way that you've clearly been using
until now.'

He wasn't commenting on the fact that it was a single
bedroom—more suitable for a child than a mother of
twins—and that the other rooms were stripped bare. 'So
tonight,' he told her firmly, 'you sleep in the bedroom and
I get the sofa.'

'But the babies…'

'That's my job,' he told her, looking down at the deep
smudges under her eyes. They looked as if they'd always
been there—the marks of absolute exhaustion—and if she
slept in the living room with everyone else then there was
no way she'd sleep soundly. 'I'll bring the babies to you
when they need a feed. If you like, I'll even change their
nappies.'

'You'll what?'

'"Greater love hath no man…"' he quipped, and then
he paused.

Silence.

Greater love… He hadn't meant to say it. It wasn't true.
Love. Ha! He didn't know the meaning of the word.

'World's greatest martyr, that's me,' he said, striving to
keep his voice light and to stop feeling the way he was
feeling about the woman in his arms. 'So enjoy being
waited on while you can. Nappy-changing—hah! I'm a

man who does what he has to do in an emergency—and then moves on fast. So in a little while I'll be gone, and I'll never be a martyr in my life again. I promise.'

'Really?' she said, looking up at him. She was very near to sleep.

'Really,' he said, and felt an almost overwhelming desire to kiss her.

It was just lucky he was a sensible man!

She slept.

Snuggled into her own bed—he'd practically undressed her again and she'd hardly objected!—she slept the moment her head hit the pillow.

Tom watched over her. First, he had watched in mock-threatening mode as she had tried to insist that he bring the cribs to her. And then, as she'd drifted into unconsciousness, he'd watched in *just* mode. *Just* because he wanted to.

He'd never stood and watched a woman sleep…

The feelings she engendered in him were weird. Her face on the pillow was pale and freckled and very, very young. Very vulnerable…that was how she looked. She made him feel protective and bossy—and very, very angry.

She was in a mess and someone must have caused it. Somewhere out there was the father of her twins. Why wasn't he looking after his lady? Tom thought, as he gazed down at her lovely face. What was that man doing leaving her in this mess?

Finally, disturbed and restless, he made his way back to the kitchen. He took Yoghurt out for her relief walk about the back garden, and then came back in to settle and watch his brood. He knew he should sleep himself, but for some reason he wasn't tired.

He was confused.

His babies slept on around him. In a strange sort of way

it was soothing, he decided, but not in a way that made
him want to sleep. He just wanted to savour it? Bottle it
for a future when he knew there would be none of this? He
settled his long frame on the sofa, trying to sort out his
thoughts. The sofa still smelled of Rose.

Rose…

He should be in Hawaii.

He didn't want to be in Hawaii. He wanted to be here.

He hadn't wanted a holiday at all, he reminded himself,
and found the tension welling up in him again. The desperation to get back to action. To fight the nightmares of
one action with another.

The memory of the last fire welled up—the noise and
the smoke and the opening of the inner chamber at the
end… The horror and the nightmares.

'Take a break,' his boss had said, and then, when he'd
refused, Charlie had taken him by the shoulders and shaken
him.

'Ten years is a long time in this game, Tom. Go find
yourself a bit of normality. You're no good to me with your
nerves shot.'

'My nerves aren't shot.'

'I can tell shot nerves when I see shot nerves and I'm
seeing 'em now. Go lie on a beach and figure out what you
want to do with your next ten years. And if you tell me
you've had enough I'll be relieved. You'll note that I don't
face burning wells any more. I have a wife and kids, and
I've learned to delegate. If you want to start delegating, it's
okay by me. Sensible, in fact. Ten years in the firing line
is enough.'

Charlie had listened to no more arguments. It was take
a holiday or be sacked, so here he was. Aching to be back.

Or was he?

Yes, he told himself firmly. Absolutely. I'd go mad stuck
permanently in a scene like this.

Another thought struck him.

'Maybe that's why Rose's husband walked out on her. Fool!

No. The place isn't making money. All this poverty...

But the farm looked great, he thought, puzzling it through in his mind. Rose's obvious poverty didn't make sense.

There was a faint whimper by the stove, and he looked over to see Yoghurt stirring. She stood. Her sleepy puppies squeaked their protest but resettled, and Yoghurt padded across to him.

'Do you want to go out, girl?' he asked, but she put her nose against his face and nuzzled.

He knew what she wanted. For heaven's sake...the dog needed a hug.

'I'm not in the affection business,' he told her, but she nuzzled again, a moist, jowly demand for contact.

Sighing, he shifted on the sofa and the great dog lumbered up right beside him. She gave him one slurpy lick, the full length of his face, and than flopped down beside him in weary affection.

'Hey, you're supposed to be with your pups.'

She cast him a reproachful look and sank closer. She had her own needs.

Yeah, right.

'Just for a minute,' he said, and found himself fondling her ears. 'Just for a minute...'

His eyes closed.

'We're not keeping up this cuddling business all night.'

He certainly wasn't.

He slept.

They all managed a reasonable night's sleep. Toby woke at three, so, figuring it was crazy to wake for one and not feed the other, Tom changed two nappies—he was getting almost professional at this!—and marched both twins in to Rose. She fed them while she was half asleep, which was just the way he wanted it.

Then, ignoring her sleepy protests, he marched them straight back to the living room and to their respective cribs. Yoghurt had decamped back to her pups, so he settled himself back on the sofa and slept until almost seven.

Once again it was Toby who acted as an alarm.

This time it wasn't as peaceful. Yoghurt needed to go outside, the puppies fretted, the nappies didn't go on as easily as they had in the middle of the night—and the contents of one nappy had him recoiling in horror. By the time he took the babies to Rose he was wide awake. He showered while she fed them, and then took tea and toast into her room.

He found her just finishing feeding, settling the babies peacefully beside her. She looked flushed and pretty, her curls tousled from sleep and her nightgown still unbuttoned from feeding. The shadows under her eyes had receded a little, he saw, and the pleasure he felt was out of all proportion to the achievement.

'Toast?' she said, startled. 'You're kidding. I don't have breakfast in bed.'

'Yoghurt just did,' he told her. 'She didn't quibble. Why should you?'

'Because I'm getting up.'

'No way. You're staying here for the day.'

'No way!'

'At least until the doctor's been.'

'I spent all yesterday in bed.'

'Nope. You spent it on the settee.'

'That's you quibbling. Not me.'

'Doesn't matter what you call it,' he said cheerfully. 'You're staying in bed regardless.' He handed over her tea and toast. 'Want me to take the twins away?'

'No.' She accepted her breakfast with grace, but then looked down at each snoozing baby. 'I'd like to keep them,' she said, and her voice was so wistful that he smiled.

'Hey, I'm not threatening to take them away from you.'

'No…'

No…

There was something in her tone—in the way she said the word—that gave him pause. He stared, and then lowered his long frame onto the end of the bed. The saggy single bed dipped even more under his weight, and the mug of tea wobbled in her hands.

Or maybe the wobble hadn't been the saggy bedsprings. Her voice had sounded wobbly too.

'Are we expecting someone to take the twins away?' he said carefully, and watched her face.

It didn't lighten. 'I… No.'

'You don't sound too certain.'

'They can't… The courts… I mean, I'm their mother.'

'Unless you maltreat them, there's no court likely to take Toby and Jess away from you,' Tom said, frowning. 'And if anyone is privy to the ghastly things your son keeps in his nappy, then there's no one who'd want them…'

She didn't smile. 'My in-laws would want them.'

'Your in-laws.'

'My husband's parents.'

'I see.' Tom frowned and concentrated. And concentrated some more. 'No,' he said finally. 'I don't see.'

She drank some tea and ate some toast. Then drank some more tea.

She didn't look at him.

'Are we going to tell Uncle Tom, then?' Tom said, and tried hard to make his face look like Uncle Tom. Avuncular… If only she weren't so darned lovely.

'It's not a very nice story.'

'You're talking to a man who faced your son's nappy,' he said. 'I'll tell you what's not very nice. Or show you! Except I buried it.'

Her eyes widened. 'Hey, those nappies aren't disposable.'

'Yes, they are. You can dispose of anything if you dig deep enough, and I disposed of it so fast you couldn't see me—or it—for dust. ''Lightning Spade'', that's me. My new nickname.'

She chuckled, but her smile didn't reach her eyes.

'Are you going to tell me?' he said.

'But—you're a stranger.' She looked doubtfully up at him, and on impulse he lifted the mug from her clasp and took her hand in his. He rubbed her fingers between his palms, feeding her warmth.

'I'm a stranger,' he agreed. 'And what you need is a friend. So how about you promote me? Just for now.'

'I...'

'Where's your husband, Rose? Where's the father of your babies?'

She took a deep breath and closed her eyes.

'He's dead.'

'Oh.' As inane remarks went, it was a beauty. Useless and inept. 'I'm sorry.'

'Don't be.'

'Rose...'

'I hated him,' she said softly— so softly, he had to lean forward to hear. The fingers between his palms clenched, and pulled away. 'I don't... He was...'

She faltered and pulled back, her eyes staring sightlessly past him.

'You know,' Tom said carefully, thinking this through, 'what we need here is sustenance. I've brought you one piece of toast and that's clearly not enough. I think this is a four-pieces-of-toast story. Each. And two more mugs of tea. Stay right where you are, Rose. Eight pieces of toast, and then you can tell me everything.'

CHAPTER FOUR

IN THE END it took almost all of Tom's huge pile of toast before she started, and when she did he had the feeling he wouldn't want to know what she told him.

So why was he listening? The Tom of two days ago would have run a mile before listening to a story like this!

But this was Rose, and she was in trouble. Just like Yoghurt. He couldn't walk away.

Just...why did it have to be him?

And the answer shot back so fast it was practically a reflex. Because he wanted it to be him.

Did he?

He didn't know, he thought savagely. His heart was telling him things his head didn't understand. He was suddenly no longer sure of anything.

But he had to listen.

'This is my farm,' she started, and Tom nodded encouragingly. This was hardly the start to a story of her husband's death, but he was in listening mode. Whatever she chose to say had to be okay by him. 'This is the bedroom I had when I was a little girl,' she went on.

That was what it still looked like, he thought, glancing around at her pretty pink curtains.

'It was your parents' farm?'

'Yes. And it's a good farm.' Her voice was curiously flat—absent—as if telling a story about someone else, or something that had happened a long time ago. 'It's viable and prosperous. I'm an only child of elderly parents. Dad died when I was sixteen but my mother and I worked it well. It was wealthy enough for us to employ a couple of men. But then, two years ago, my mother died.'

'I'm sorry.'

'Don't be. It was time. She was pleased in the end—that she was going to Dad.'

'And then?'

Still she was absent, talking mechanically. He had the feeling that at any minute she'd turn off the switch, and he had to find out as much as he could before then.

Rose shrugged. 'Then—nothing. I mean nothing. I hadn't realized how isolated we'd become. While my mother was ill I nursed her, and she needed me here all the time. So there was the farm and my mother and nothing else. After she died my farm manager left to go overseas, so I took on someone else, but I hardly knew him. I was working solidly and grieving for my mother and not seeing many people my own age…'

'So…'

'So I was a sitting duck,' she said bitterly, and for the first time there was emotion. Raw, blinding pain. 'A naive little fool who fell for the first good-looking face…'

'Your husband.'

'Chris was thirty, the indulged youngest son of wealthy graziers north of here. He was charming, happy—he made me laugh and you can't know how much I wanted to laugh. He seemed wealthy in his own right. He swept me off my feet, and of course it made sense that we'd live here when we were married. I mean, his older brother stood to inherit his father's farm, and he loved farming. Or he said he did.'

'But he didn't.'

'He lied.' Rose took a deep breath. 'Chris was one big lie. He was in debt up to his neck. He was a compulsive gambler. He'd lost his job as a stock and station agent, and gone through so much of his parents' money that they'd stopped supplying him with more. But still he was in debt, dangerously in debt, to the point where his creditors were starting to threaten—and he didn't have very nice creditors.'

'But surely—'

'I was too blind—too much in love to see,' she continued bitterly. 'I loved the farm. I loved being out on the horses, and with the cattle. Chris offered to take over the business side of things and I trusted him. So I signed...' She sighed. 'Well, I won't bore you with all the stupid details, but it's enough to say I signed things I was stupid to sign and ended up as committed to his debt as he was. And then it all came out. He wanted the farm. That's why he'd married me. If I sold the farm, he'd clear his debt.'

'But you—'

'I'd be left with nothing.'

Tom took a deep breath. Not pretty! 'So...?' he prodded when she fell into silence. He had to know it all now.

'Maybe I would have done it,' she said bleakly. 'Sold the farm, I mean. Everything was a mess and I went to my lawyer and he said it'd be a protracted legal nightmare to get out of it. So I figured that I'd been stupid and so I'd pay the price for my stupidity. I'd walk away with nothing, but at least I'd be free of Chris. But then—' she grimaced '—then I found I was pregnant.'

'Oh, Rose.'

'"Oh, Rose" is right,' she said bleakly. 'Of all the silly fools! I was in debt up to my ears, I had a husband who was still gambling, and I couldn't walk away from the farm because...the farm didn't seem mine. Once I was pregnant, that is. It belonged to my parents and my grandparents and my great-grandparents before that. Four generations. It seemed like it was all I had to give to my children—their heritage—all they would have. After all, I already knew that I couldn't give them a father.'

'He didn't love you?'

'He married me to get the farm,' she said, and there was such harshness in her voice that he believed her. 'Then, when I found out, the night I realised I was pregnant, another woman came looking for Chris—abusing him for breaking promises he'd made, after we were married.'

'He sounds,' Tom said carefully, 'like the world's greatest scumbag.'

'He was that,' Rose said. 'And more.'

'So you kicked him out?'

'Not straight away.' Her face lightened a little, thinking back. 'I was so angry. So humiliated. The fact that I was pregnant—and the other woman coming here—that cleared my head a bit. Got me into fighting mode. I headed straight back to my lawyer—Mr Lett's an old friend of my father's and we sat up most of the night thinking things through.'

'He helped you…'

'I told him everything. There was only one thing going for me—the farm was still in my name. There were vast debts in my name, too, so I couldn't keep the farm, but I was angry enough by then not to hand it to Chris's creditors. So I signed it away. Mr Lett set it up in a trust for my children. I no longer own the farm. The twins do. Then I arranged to file for legal separation from Chris, and to declare myself bankrupt, and I went home to tell Chris what I'd done.'

'I can imagine,' Tom said carefully, 'that he wasn't pleased.'

'What do you think?'

'You were providing for his children.'

'He didn't see them as *his* children,' Rose said bitterly. 'He saw them as a hindrance. He got drunk and told me…he told me there'd be no babies. And he bashed me.'

'Rose!'

'It might have worked,' Rose said sadly, 'but Mr Lett

was worried about me, and he thought he'd drop by to check. He walked in on a really ugly scene. Chris took off. I ended up in hospital—for a while they thought I might lose the twins anyway—and Chris smashed his car and died. I'm not sure whether it was suicide or whether one of his creditors caused the smash—or whether he just got too drunk to care. Whatever, he died. End of story.'

'It's a pretty ghastly story.'

'It is, isn't it?' she said, managing a smile. 'Then—his parents blamed me. They hate me. They knew what he was, but it was easier to blame me than to blame their dead son. They've offered to take the twins. Threatened, really. They say I can't look after them when I don't have any money. And the neighbours... Chris borrowed money from so many of them, and now they see me still living on the farm when they think it should be sold to pay them off. Only I didn't borrow the money. And I don't see why—'

'Hey, Rose, it's okay.'

'It's not okay,' she said savagely. 'I should repay them and I will, but I'll have to do it slowly. I won't sell the children's farm. I can't now, even if I wanted to, so, right or wrong, I'm stuck.' She raised her eyes to his, trying to read in his face that he understood. That he didn't condemn her. As if he could! 'But, Tom, I don't—I don't tell this story often. In fact, you're the first—' Her voice broke.

'Rose.'

It was too much. He moved forward and hauled her into his arms, cradling her against his chest. She felt good there. Right. As if she belonged. And the feelings she created in him were threatening to overwhelm him.

'Rose, life's a cow but there's always tomorrow,' he said softly, stroking her hair, and she hiccuped and pulled back in his arms.

'There is,' she agreed defiantly.

'You want a handkerchief?'

'No. I'm not crying.' She gave an emphatic sniff.

'I can see that.' Ha!

'I'm normally fine. I don't cry. I refuse to let it get to me.'

'This is probably post-natal depression kicking in,' he said kindly. 'You're allowed ten minutes of it.'

'Ten minutes!'

'Single babies, five. Twins, ten.'

'Says who?'

'The Dr Bradley School of Maternal Care,' he said sagely. 'It's the same manual that tells me to bury dirty nappies.'

She choked, but this time it was on a chuckle.

'You're crazy.'

'Yep. And you're broke. And I've eaten too much breakfast and someone has to do the washing-up and the sun's come out. Everything in perspective, Rose Allen?'

'Everything in perspective,' she managed, and her smile stayed. It was lop-sided and watery, but it was still there. 'Can I get up and help with the dishes?'

'No way in the wide world,' he told her. 'The Tom Bradley Domestic Service is in full swing. It's never operated before and may never operate again, so enjoy it while you can, madam. Lie back and enjoy your babies. And hope they end up nice kids.'

'Of course they'll end up nice kids. Why wouldn't they?'

'They'll be rich as nabobs. I'm sure giving kids farms before they're even born comes under the category of spoiling them rotten. What will you give them for their first birthday? The moon?'

And he escaped while she was still chuckling—and while he still had the capacity to escape without hauling her back into his arms.

He was nuts.

Rose lay back on her pillows and gazed out at the morning light over the paddocks. The cattle were grazing peacefully in the sun. Her babies snoozed on, tucked in beside her.

All was right with her world. For the moment. Thanks to Tom.

What would she have done with him?

She hated to think. The bleakness she'd faced before the babies' birth had been put aside. Tom had brought peace and laughter and happiness into her house. Instead of an empty kitchen, she had a dog and seven puppies and a man whistling silly tunes while he did the washing-up.

She didn't know the first thing about him. She should send him away, she told herself, but she was doing no such thing.

You always were a fool when it came to men, Rose Allen, said an inner voice.

Once. Just once.

So what are you doing letting this man into your life? You thought you knew everything about Chris and yet you know even less about this man.

Tom's kind.

He was more than that. She raised her hand to her cheek—her hand that he'd held. It still smelled faintly of him. Or maybe that was post-nappy and baby powder...

She grinned, thinking of him marching off down the paddocks with his spade. What a hero!

A hero. That was what he was, she decided sleepily as she snuggled back down into her pillows with her babies. She should fight him. She should dress herself and march out to send him away—and be independent and alone.

But for now it was too delicious to be warm and cared for and...and cherished.

By a hero—whoever he was!

'I want to slug someone but he's dead,' Tom told Yoghurt as he cleared the breakfast things. 'Have you ever felt like that?'

Yoghurt looked at him.

'Yeah, and while I'm at it I wouldn't mind a shot at the creep who called you Yoghurt.'

Yoghurt's big head drooped. As looks went, Yoghurt's was a winner. Sort of a combination of agreement, pathos, desperation and longing. Her message was clear as a bell.

'Toast not enough, huh?'

Yoghurt's head lifted and her tail moved a smidgen. Not much, but definitely more than Tom had seen it move before. He was definitely on the right track here.

'There are eggs in the fridge.'

The tail moved more.

'Hey, this is easy,' Tom said, grinning and reaching for the fridge door. 'One eggnog, coming up. Why didn't I think of that before?'

And then his smile died again.

'Now if only I could figure out how to make the lady happy as well.'

He had a feeling it wouldn't be nearly as easy.

The doctor arrived mid-afternoon—about two minutes after the phone came on line—and by the time he came Tom felt as if he ought to be in apron and curlers. He'd checked the cows again, but the rest of the day had been taken up with domesticity. He'd swept and laundered and changed the odd score of nappies and had been immersed in housework up to his ears.

Now he ushered the doctor in and was feeling so domestic that it was all he could do not to say, Wipe your feet, as the doctor crossed the threshold.

The man was elderly, efficient and brusque, and came right to the point.

'Who the hell are you?' he demanded as he stepped inside.

'Tom Bradley,' Tom said, trying to look respectable. Housemaid-like.

'Friend of Rose's?'

'Um…yes.'

The doctor subjected him to a long stare, his greying eyebrows beetling. Finally he offered a faint smile—conditional approval.

'Glad to hear it,' he growled. 'The girl's lacking a few friends. She should be surrounded now, instead of which she's been sent to Coventry. All because of that dratted husband of hers. Staying long?'

'Um…' Tom didn't appreciate the doctor's stare. He felt like something on the dissecting table—any minute now the doctor would figure out what species he was. The sort that didn't commit… 'I'm not sure.'

'Just until she's on her feet again,' the doctor said encouragingly.

'Um…'

'Good lad.' He gave Tom a hearty clap on the shoulder and the gruff old doctor headed for Rose. He could tell where she was. Toby—of course it was Toby—was awake and telling the world it was time for tea.

Tom was left to his housework.

They were all pronounced fine.

'Damned healthy babies. Damned healthy mother,' Tom was told when he was called in after the examination. 'You've done well.'

'I didn't do a thing,' Tom said, reddening. 'I just caught them.'

'And didn't interfere. Lots of home-birthers go poking where nature never intended anyone to poke. End up with infection all over the place. And Rose tells me you kept her calm throughout. Kept her from panicking. That's the main thing.' He packed his instruments with brisk efficiency. 'Okay. The wee ones need a couple of tests done—there are blood tests we give all newborns—but they can wait until next week. By the sound of those lungs, there's no need for worry.'

'But I can get up, can't I?' Rose said. She cast a baleful look at Tom. 'Tom won't let me.'

'Tom's a sensible lad, but there's no need to stay in bed.'

'There.'

'As long as you do nothing,' he continued. 'And that means nothing. You'll lift nothing heavier than a baby for at least ten days, and even then ten wet nappies in a wash basket's the maximum you can lift at once.'

'But—'

'And that means no hay bales, Rose Allen,' the doctor said warningly, fixing her with a look that meant business. 'Not even half a hay bale.'

'I wouldn't—'

'You'll be hand-feeding, won't you?' the doctor demanded, turning to Tom. 'Everyone else in the district is.'

'Hand-feeding?' Tom was lost.

'I am,' Rose said in distress. 'But of course I haven't for the last couple of days. It won't have hurt for the cattle to go without until now, but...'

'I didn't know we were hand-feeding,' Tom said carefully. 'Why didn't you tell me we were hand-feeding, Rose?'

'*We* aren't. *I* am.'

'*We* are.' Tom glared at her. 'Shut up, Rose, or I'll stop doing nappy duty.'

'Nappy duty! Your idea of nappy duty is to bury them once they're dirty!' She practically bounced in indignation. 'How many nappies do I have left?'

'Enough.'

'I'll bet I haven't.'

'I'll bet you have,' Tom said virtuously, showing off in front of the doctor. 'I found a cupboard full of towels and a pair of scissors. Come the revolution, we'll still have enough nappies to clothe the multitudes. The loaves and fishes have nothing on me!'

Rose choked and the old doctor grinned. He took Tom's hand and wrung it.

'I can see I'm leaving her in safe hands. Well done. I'll leave you to it. Ring me if you need me, boy, but if you keep her quiet…'

'She keeps arguing,' Tom said plaintively. 'I'm sure it's not good for her. Can you tell her quiet means compliant?'

'Compliant in Rose Allen means sick,' the doctor said, chuckling. 'And we wouldn't want that, now, would we?'

'No,' said Tom, and sighed. He looked down at Rose and smiled. 'I guess we wouldn't.'

And Rose looked up into that smile and she couldn't resist smiling back—and the doctor left with all sorts of ideas forming in his wise old head.

'So tell me about hand-feeding.'

'It's nothing. You can't…'

'I can,' Tom said. 'Of course I can. That's what I'm here for.'

Rose lay back on the pillows and gazed up at him, baffled. What on earth was making this man tick? And—who was he?

'I think,' she said carefully, 'that it's time you told me about you.'

'Such as what?' Tom eyed her warily. 'Yoghurt needs a walk.'

'Are you a bank robber on the run?'

'No!'

'I wouldn't mind,' she said carefully. 'I mean—I'm so

grateful. I'd probably even condone a crime or two. As long as it wasn't violent.'

'Now that's nice of you,' Tom said, grinning.

'So if I was, say, guilty of forging a few cheques?'

'I guess I'd forgive…'

'Or robbing a few old ladies of their life's savings?'

'Maybe not.' She fixed him with a baleful look. 'Maybe I wouldn't give you up to the law, but I'd ask you to leave.'

'And tell the law where I'd gone?'

'I might be vague.'

'And if I mugged an accomplice in crime—took his share of the loot?'

Why was she so sure he was guilty of nothing of the kind? Rose looked up into his deep-set, twinkly eyes and knew for sure this man was honest. Absolutely honest!

'If you mugged him then he probably deserved it,' she said. 'Can I share the loot?'

He hooted with laughter. 'That'd make you an accessory after the fact.'

'Probably. Is it comfortable in prison?'

'You mean, speaking from my long experience behind bars?'

It was her turn to chuckle, but as he smiled and made to leave, her hand came out and caught him. It was an unconscious gesture, her fingers reaching out to detain him, but it caught him like an electric shock.

He stood stock-still and stared down.

'Tom, tell me.'

'Tell you what?' His voice came out stiff and unnatural.

'Tell me why you're running?'

'I'm not running.'

'Yes, you are,' she said softly. 'I can see it in your face. There's something…'

'My buried bank heist accomplice,' he said flippantly, but she didn't smile.

'I don't think so.'

'What about my wife and ten kids, then? he said, and grimaced dramatically. 'I can't take any more. One more session of *Sesame Street…*'

'I think,' she said carefully, 'that you'd very much enjoy *Sesame Street*.'

'I do, but too much of a good thing.'

'So who's Oscar?'

'Oscar?'

'Yes.' Her hand gripped tighter as he tried to pull away. Like the old doctor, she had him pinned on her dissecting table and there was no room for him to wriggle free. 'Oscar.'

'Everyone knows who Oscar is,' he said loftily.

'The frog?'

'Yeah. Oscar the Frog.'

'Mmm—' she smirked '—I knew it. You have no more idea of *Sesame Street* than you have of hand-feeding cattle. I knew it the minute I saw your nappies.'

'What's wrong with my nappies?' he asked, offended, and in answer Rose lifted tiny Jessie from the bed. Jessie snoozed on. Rose unwrapped her woolly blanket and held her daughter out.

One saggy nappy drooped downwards—and landed in a heap on the bed.

'Real professionalism, that.' Rose cast him a twinkling smile, removing any offence from her words. 'Not that I'm complaining, mind.'

'You'd better not be.'

'Or you'll head off in high dudgeon?'

'That's right!'

'To where?' she asked softly, settling her daughter again, tightening the offending nappy and rewrapping.

'To where I was heading before I met you head-on.'

'Which was?'

'Hawaii.'

'And why were you going to Hawaii?'

'On holiday. Is this inquisition nearly over?'

'Nope. You still know more about me than I do about you and it isn't fair. So you missed your plane because of me.'

'Because of me,' he said sternly, looking down at her and trying not to connect to those searching eyes. She saw too much. 'Because I crashed the car.'

'Because of Yoghurt, then. It wasn't your fault so don't you dare say it was. Do you have friends meeting you in Hawaii?'

'No.'

'So you're a loner.'

'That's the one.'

'Like me,' she said gently. 'What do you do for a living, Tom Bradley?'

'I put out oil-well fires.'

That startled her. 'You're kidding.'

'No.'

'You mean...' She frowned, thinking it through. 'How many oil-well fires are there likely to be in this country at any one time?'

'In this country?'

'Yes.'

He grinned at that. 'Well, maybe none. I'm international.'

'Oh, right. I see. It's a case of "have extinguisher, will travel"!'

'That's the one.'

There was silence while she thought this through. She shouldn't believe him, she thought, staring up at him, but there was something in his face—there was the echo of trouble.

She did believe him.

'It's dangerous, isn't it?' she asked, and he nodded.

'Sometimes. Mostly not. I guess it's ninety per cent boredom, ten per cent panic.'

'Why are you on holiday?'

'A man needs—'

'I thought men like you would be on call all the time,' she said, her intelligent mind sorting it through. 'I mean— you'd have your holidays when there aren't fires. But you're not even carrying a mobile phone.'

She was getting too close to the bone, here. Tom backed off a notch or two in his mind, mentally closing her out. 'I needed a rest.'

'Something happened.'

'Something always happens.'

But she knew. She saw. 'Want to tell me about it?'

He shook his head and his face closed. Absolutely. 'No.'

'I told you my trauma.'

'You wouldn't want to know mine,' he said—he'd meant it to sound light, but instead it came out grim and rough.

'So…' She lay back with her twins and checked him out, her eyes not leaving his. Searching for something she didn't quite understand. 'Let's see what we have here. An adventurer who needed to get away from adventure.'

'My boss ordered me…'

'That bad, huh?'

'Hey, Rose.'

'Okay.' She held up her hands in defeat. 'I won't ask anything else. Except one thing.'

He sighed. 'What?'

'You're international, right?'

'Yes.'

'So why are you here?' I mean, on this piece of road at this time. Right at this moment, there are no oil-well fires in the whole country—as far as I know.'

He sighed again. 'Very perceptive,' he said dryly. 'I've been visiting my mother.'

'But not—' her eyes read his mind '—not to stay with her.'

'Hey, I stayed for a night.' And that was a night too long, he thought grimly as he was forced back to face those all-seeing eyes.

'You don't get along?'

'That's another question and you said only one more.'

'So I did,' she said slowly. 'Okay. End of inquisition. But I'm starting to think...'

'You're starting to think what, Rose Allen?' he demanded. 'You're starting to think too much!'

'The doctor didn't say to stop thinking.' She peeped a smile at him, humour resurfacing. 'And I'm thinking I should lose my guilt trip.'

'Why?'

'Because something tells me that you need this place almost as much as I need you, Tom Bradley,' she said softly. 'Something tells me that, for the next couple of weeks, we're made for each other!'

Which was all very well, Tom thought as he dug out the same dratted cow again the next day—and the day after that. The dopy bovine kept heading for the water-hole the same way. Maybe Rose was right. Maybe a few weeks of digging out cows and hauling hay bales and juggling babies and puppies were just what the doctor ordered.

He was certainly sleeping better than he had for months—years! By the time he fell into bed at night he was exhausted, and every night Yoghurt hauled herself up into his bed and licked him goodnight.

Affection and domesticity were closing in on him from all sides. Sleep was the only escape!

It always had been, but until now there'd always been

the risk of nightmares. Now, before the nightmares had a chance to catch up with him, a twin would wake and he'd stir and carry an armful of babies into Rose's room—and sit and watch her feed.

Maybe have her tease him a little. Maybe cuddle a twin while the other one took longer to feed.

It was like a drug, he thought warily as the days wore on. A sweet, hypnotic drug that had the power to seduce a man's mind.

To make him forget he was a man alone.

Which he was. He couldn't let himself forget that for a minute!

CHAPTER FIVE

THEY had five days before the world broke in, and in those five days even Yoghurt seemed to thrive. The big dog grew more placid by the day. Her flanks filled out, her puppies grew into fat, glossy little worms—still blind but growing more active. The twins settled into a reasonable routine, and so did Tom and Rose.

They needed groceries. A steady diet of pasta was getting monotonous! They needed to get the truck fixed, but Tom, hauling hay across the paddocks by hand-cart, was strangely reluctant to call in the tow-truck and have it fixed. For now, the world could wait.

In the end it was a shock to hear a knock on the porch door early on Friday afternoon. Tom opened it to find a middle-aged lady standing before him, her expression grimly determined. She was holding a large casserole dish, and she held it out as if it were physically hurting her to hand it over.

'This is for Rose—because of the babies.'

'Come in and give it to her yourself,' Tom said mildly, pulling the door open wide.

'No.' There was clipped anger in the word.

'Can I ask why not?'

The woman gave an angry gasp. 'Doc Connor said we weren't being kindly, the way we were treating her. Said she was all alone with twins. But she's not alone. She has you and that ought to be enough. I might have known she'd have another man. I should just take my casserole away again.'

She turned, but couldn't leave. Tom's hand was gripping her arm, and his expression was icy.

'I think,' he said calmly, so calmly that anyone who knew him would have backed off fast, 'that you need to explain yourself.'

The woman drew in a hissing breath. 'I shouldn't have come.'

'But you're here. So now you'll tell me.' Tom led her right out onto the porch and shut the door behind him. He didn't want Rose within earshot. 'Now!'

'You can't—'

'I can,' he said, putting on a scowl. He wasn't all that good at intimidation, but this was easy. She was looking at him like a petrified rabbit. For heaven's sake, what was the woman expecting? That he'd keep her here in chains until she told all?

Gee, her casserole smelled good…

Enough of that. Back to threatening mode. 'You know, there are things going on here that I don't understand,' he said coldly. 'Maybe it's time I knew.'

'I don't have to tell you anything. If Rose has another man—'

'I'm not Rose's man,' Tom snapped, with a quick glance at the open window behind them. As long as she couldn't hear…'I'm Rose's friend, and it seems to me that she's being treated unfairly by the whole valley!'

'She…being treated unfairly—it's us!' The woman clenched her lips tight together and wrenched away, but Tom wasn't going to let her. He grabbed the casserole—some things were important!—and placed it tenderly on the porch step, and then he took hold of the woman's shoulders and sat her forcibly beside it.

'Tell me,' he said.

'Tell you what?' she demanded angrily.

'Tell me what Rose has done to hurt you.'

'Oh, for heaven's sake, you must know—'

'Only what Rose has told me.' Tom softened his tone and flashed her his very nicest smile—the smile that usually worked a treat where women were concerned. It didn't fail him now. The woman cast him a strange glance and despite herself her face puckered into an uncertain smile in response. His smile really was a winner!

'She really hasn't told you?'

'No. You tell me.'

'If you really don't know...well, you be careful.'

'Why would I need to be careful?'

'She's a cheat and she owes everyone money,' the woman said. 'Right, left and centre. All over the valley. The Allens have always been rich. This is one of the biggest farms in the district. Rose's family have an excellent reputation, so when she asked us to invest—'

'Hey, whoa,' Tom said. 'Rose asked you to invest?'

'Well, not directly, but that nice young husband of hers said she had it all set up. She was organizing us into an artificial insemination programme, from imported blood-stock, but doing it as a co-operative. He said she had it all worked out. It costs so much to bring *in vitro* material into the country, so Rose said it'd be cheaper if we did it as a group! We all put money up front—thousands and thousands—and look where it got us.'

'Where did it get you?'' Tom asked mildly, and he was told!

'Nowhere. Nothing.' The words came out as a furious accusation. 'Not one cow ever became pregnant through her crazy scheme, because the money disappeared before it was paid to the importers. We started asking questions and Chris said—he said she was kicking him out and she'd invested our money overseas. Not in the scheme at all. He was so ashamed that he killed himself. The police were trying to find him because of a crazy accusation she had made, and he was so desperate he drove into a tree.

'And now she's left with the farm—there's some legal strings she's pulled which mean she doesn't have to sell it—and I bet she has all the money in the world in overseas banks and the like… And I don't know why I'm bringing her a casserole except perhaps it's because those kiddies of hers are really partly his, and he was such a nice boy and maybe he'd want us to take an interest. Until his parents can get them away from her.'

She sniffed an angry sniff and would have risen, but Tom's hands came out and pressed her down again.

'I have to go,' she protested.

'Sit,' he said in a voice that brooked no opposition. 'Tell me where you heard all this. That it was Rose whose scheme it was.'

'Why, from Chris, of course,' the woman said. 'Her poor husband. I told you. She set it up and he was conned. And after he died—well, we couldn't get near *her* to ask any questions. We all got little notes enclosing money—a paltry sum compared with what we're owed—and a promise that she'd pay as soon as she could, but the amount was ridiculous. She locked herself up and wouldn't speak to anyone. Then Chris's parents—they're lovely people—they told us what happened. She lured him in. He did all the dirty work without realising what was happening, and she's left with the cash.'

'What's your name?' Tom demanded suddenly, and the woman started.

'Joan. Joan Mitchell.'

'Mrs Mitchell, look about you,' Tom insisted. 'Tell me what you see.'

The woman looked. 'What? I don't see anything. What am I supposed to be seeing?'

'Maybe fancy cars?' Tom said. 'Horses? Fences in good

condition? New equipment? Anything that suggests money.'

There was nothing. Of course there was nothing. Out in front of the house Rose's sad old truck sagged on its damaged wheel, looking for all the world as if it was about to sink into the mud. The driveway underneath it had been chewed up by the exposed wheel-rim, but it had been potholed before. This farm was a beautiful place, but it was plainly down at the heel.

'She hides it,' the woman said stubbornly.

'There are fabulous stables here,' Tom said softly. 'They show every evidence of there being horses here until recently. Lots of horses.'

'The Allens have always had horses! Rose practically rode before she could walk. She loves them.'

'She doesn't have them now,' Tom said sadly. 'There's not a horse on the place. There's not a vehicle except for this one. There are only two furnished rooms in the house. All the rest of the furniture has been sold. Rose is living on eggs and pasta, and her babies are dressed in the cheapest clothes she could find.'

The woman stared. 'I don't believe it.'

'Believe it,' Tom said harshly.

'But where did the money go?'

'To that charming young man who died,' Tom told her, grimly determined. There was no earthly reason why this woman shouldn't know the truth. If Rose hadn't told them, then someone should. 'He killed himself, not from shame but because he'd bashed his wife, he was dead broke and both the police and the loan sharks were after him. He had massive gambling debts he'd run up before he married Rose. He married her so she'd be forced to sell the farm and pay them off. She sold everything, but the farm itself is in trust for her children. She can't sell that—and neither could he.'

'I don't believe it,' the woman gasped.

'Don't you?'

For the first time she looked uneasy. The middle-aged woman stared up at Tom and he gazed calmly back. Then her eyes shifted to the truck again. 'That's all she's got?' she asked, and her voice had dropped a notch or two. The anger was dissipating while he watched.

'That's all she has.'

'She never said…'

'That her husband was a cheat and a liar? Would you?'

'But his parents—they say it was her fault. They say she won't be a fit mother.'

'So as well as being robbed blind she now has the threat of her babies being taken away from her,' Tom said ruthlessly. 'And the rest of the neighbourhood think she's a swindler. I'd say she's had it rough, wouldn't you?'

'Oh, my dear…' The woman stared blankly out over the farm, taking in the enormity of what she'd been told. 'She's never said anything.'

'No.'

Joan Mitchell looked up into his face, her eyes reflecting her uncertainty. 'You're sure?'

'I'm sure.'

'But Doc Connor must have known—he always said we should find out the facts before we judged, but we thought…well, Chris's parents told us…'

'And you believed them.' Tom's voice gentled. 'I guess I don't blame you. They were distraught at losing their son. They'd lash out at anyone—and to believe he could do that…'

'But she went away. She didn't even come to the funeral.'

That was when the damage had really been done, Tom thought bleakly. A charming young man had died. There was a neighbourhood of people who were owed money, there were grieving, angry parents, and Rose had not been there to defend herself. And probably she had had too much pride to tell everyone what her husband had done.

'She was in hospital,' Tom told the woman, and there was no way she could fail to believe him now. His voice was implacable. 'He bashed her, you see. When he found that the farm was in trust for his unborn children and that he couldn't sell it, then he tried to get rid of them. When he couldn't, and with the kinds of creditors he had, he killed himself. But how could Rose face you after that? How could she face herself?'

'You told her what?' Rose sat up on the couch with a jolt. 'Tom Bradley, you had no right.'

'No. Neither did your doctor or your lawyer and so they didn't. But me—there's no medical or legal code binding me to silence. I'm damned if I'll stand by and let them think you're the villain of the piece. So I set her right.'

'You told her everything?'

'Everything. And now she wants to see you.'

'Tom, I can't,' she wailed. 'I don't know how! No one's been near me since Chris died. How can I face them now?'

'She's outside waiting, and you have to face people some time,' Tom told her gently. He crossed to the settee and gripped her shoulders. 'This is just the start. You need to make a life for yourself and your babies, Rose, love, and this is the beginning.'

Rose, love... The unfamiliar endearment drifted around the room, warming her to the core. *Rose, love*... No one had called her that since her father had died.

'Tom...' Her voice faltered to silence.

'Starting now.' He smiled down into her confused eyes, and his smile was enough to make her still—to calm the jumble of emotion tumbling through her heart. *Rose, love*...

'She's coming in and she's staying,' he was saying, 'for three hours.'

'Three hours!'

'Three hours,' he told her sternly. 'And she's lending me her car.'

'What—what are you going to do?'

'Me?' He grinned, a grin so wide it split his face. 'Can't you guess? I'm going shopping!'

'Rose?'

The woman at the door was hesitant, looking into the kitchen as if she expected a bullet rather than a welcome. Joan Mitchell was Rose's closest neighbour. She'd been a friend to Rose's mother, but Chris had robbed her family of thousands they could ill afford.

'Mrs. Mitchell.' Rose started to rise, but the little woman came beetling across the room as if she'd been blown in from behind.

'Oh, my dear, don't you dare stand up for me. Is it true?' She stopped and stared around her, her sharp eyes taking everything in. 'Rose! Your mother's antiques! The china set on the dresser. The lovely rocker. They're not here any more. You've sold everything!' She burst into tears and gathered Rose to her. 'Oh, Rose, we've been so cruel, and I hear you have such lovely babies. Twins, the doctor says, a boy and a girl, and I haven't even brought you baby gifts.'

'But she's brought a casserole,' Tom said encouragingly from behind. He cast Rose a wicked grin as Rose looked desperately up at him over the distraught lady. 'I see I'm leaving you in capable hands, Rose, dear. Goodbye, ladies. I'll be back in time for dinner. There's no pasta in your casserole, is there, Joan?'

'No, but—'

'Then that settles it,' he said cheerfully. 'I'll definitely be back.'

Tom Bradley was not a man to shop. He bought what he must when he must, and that was that. But now he approached town with a great buzz of anticipation.

First things first. He headed to the garage where his car had been taken, shook his head over the wreck, made a few phone calls and organized another hire car. Or, rather, a hire truck. Hand-feeding by cart was the pits!

Then he hit the shops as if he meant business.

First the supermarket. Tom filled a trolley to overflowing, wheeled it to the astounded check-out girl, and parked it beside her.

'I'll be back,' he told her, and took off with an empty trolley. Hey, this was fun!

Three trolleys later he was out of there, and his stomach was already rumbling in anticipation of the food he'd bought. If he never saw pasta again, he wouldn't mind in the least.

Four o'clock.

He had another hour before the shops closed, and he was a man with a mission. He grinned and headed off down the street with his credit card burning a hole in his pocket.

'So who's Tom?' Joan Mitchell was scratching around the kitchen like a mother hen, making up in cluckiness now for her coldness over the past eight months.

'A friend.'

'A friend of the family? Or a friend of yours?'

'There is only me and the twins now, so I guess you could say he's a friend of the family.'

'But your parents knew him?'

'He hasn't been here for a very long time,' Rose hedged, and that seemed to satisfy Joan.

'He's a single man?'

'I...yes.' She was pretty sure about that. She was definitely sure he didn't have children, and by the way he backed away from emotion she figured he couldn't have a wife.

'That's nice, dear,' Joan said complacently, and Rose cast her a startled look.

'Hey, it's not like that.'

'You mean he's not nutty on you?'

'No!'

'Mmm.' Joan looked over at Rose and smiled. 'Maybe not. But if he was…'

'I'm not in the market for a relationship,' Rose said bitterly. 'Once bitten, twice shy.'

'Just because you hit on one bad egg it doesn't mean the whole basket is bad,' Joan said sternly. 'My Bob's just lovely.'

Rose thought of Bob Mitchell and couldn't suppress a smile. Bob was about four foot eight high, about the same wide, he was bald as a nut and he was bossed unmercifully by his wife.

But she thought he was lovely. Rose felt her insides clench in what could only be envy.

'Mmm.'

'And that smile…' Joan sighed romantically, still focused right on Tom. She might love her Bob but that didn't stop her appreciating others. 'Well, with a smile like that… If I was your age and a man like that asked to put his boots under my bed…'

'Joan Mitchell!'

'Just don't look a gift horse in the mouth, will you, dear?' she said sternly. 'These babies of yours need a daddy.'

'They had a daddy,' Rose said sadly.

'And he was a dud. Go find them another. Or, rather, don't go anywhere. Just stay where you are and let events take their course.'

'He's not the least bit interested in me—in that way.'

'That's hogwash, dear,' Joan said complacently. 'I think I might even send my Bob over to ask his intentions.'

'Joan Mitchell, don't you dare!'

'You don't have parents, Rose,' Joan told her. 'Someone has to look after you.'

'Tom will.' The words were out before she could help herself and she gasped as she heard them. And Joan's grin widened by a country mile.

'That's exactly what I meant, my dear,' she said happily. 'That's just the way I'm thinking it should be.'

Tom reached home at dusk, just as Joan was starting to get edgy about her darling Bob's dinner. She would have loved to stay to find out what was in his heap of parcels, but Tom had organised the hire truck to follow him so that Joan could run the driver back to town.

'It's the least you can do,' he told her wickedly when she demurred at the half-hour trip. 'You've treated Rose abysmally. This is your afternoon of atonement.'

He smiled down at her, she cast an exasperated look up at him—but he was smiling and she was lost. There was no way you could fail to respond when this young man was being charming.

'You look after her,' she said weakly as he ushered her into her car.

'Oh, I will,' Tom promised. He closed the door firmly on her and raised his hand in farewell. 'I will.'

'Food!'

Rose stood at the kitchen table and gaped as bag after bag of groceries was hauled into her kitchen. She'd never seen so many groceries in her life!

'You bet, food.'

'We don't need...'

'We do need.'

'Tom, I can't afford…'

'I can.'

'But why?' She practically wailed, staring helplessly as he carried bag after bag inside. 'Tom you don't need to be here any more. I have my neighbours. You've done so much.'

'I can't leave until my car is fixed,' he told her.

'You were catching a plane.'

'So I was. But I'm very attached to my little car.'

'Really?'

'Really.'

It didn't make sense. None of it made sense, but Rose watched as Tom transferred his day's shopping into the house and she knew that she wouldn't question it all too closely. Okay, she should send him on his way, but…

What had Joan said? If a man like that put his boots under her bed…

She blushed scarlet and had to lean over a crib to hide her face from Tom. She was being ridiculous!

It was just that she was lonely, she told herself firmly. In the last eight months she had been so isolated that she'd thought she'd go mad. And now here was this personable whirlwind of a man, making her laugh, filling her house with his smile.

It would seem so empty when he finally went.

So, he should go—but if he didn't want to go quite yet— well, she wasn't the one to push!

Dinner was just plain magnificent. 'It's a birthday dinner,' Tom told her, setting the table with a flourish. 'The twins' birthday.'

'That was almost a week ago.'

'Did we have a birthday dinner then? Surely not. All I remember is pasta.'

'No, but—'

'No, we didn't have a party. So we're having a party now. Sit down, shut up and enjoy.'

'You're not cooking!' she had protested.

'I can cook,' he had replied, wounded. 'Just watch!'

He could, too, if you called cooking heating Joan's casserole as entrée, searing steak and tossing salad as main course and then hulling strawberries for dessert. Still, Rose decided as she drank home-brewed coffee and ate rum truffles, it was about the best meal she'd eaten in her life—heaven, she'd been living on pasta for so long!

She wasn't the only one to appreciate Tom's groceries. So did Yoghurt!

The big dog looked up wearily as Tom came towards her with her dinner bowl—and then got a whiff of what was inside. The world's biggest rump steak! She stood up so fast that her puppies fell from her teats in confusion.

'Some things are more important than motherhood.' Tom grinned down at the dog as she attacked her steak as if her life depended on it. 'I think we should change your name.'

Yoghurt cast him one adoring glance—with her mouth full—then went right back to eating.

'What will you do with her?' Tom asked mildly, watching the dog with affection. 'When I'm gone?'

'I—' That caught her unawares. Rose set down her cup and stared into the dregs. *When I'm gone*...

'I guess she can stay.'

'Where are your farm dogs?'

'I only had one,' she said. 'Polly. The night Chris bashed me she...well, she tried to defend me.'

Enough said. The look on Rose's face told him the rest.

'So now you have eight farm dogs,' Tom said cheerfully, carrying her plate to the sink. 'They might need a bit of training.'

'I don't know...'

'Hey, they might be really suited to the job. Eight blood-

hounds! They'll sure be able to find your cows, even if
they won't know what to do with them when they've found
them.' He grinned at her stunned look, then hauled a box
from the floor. He still had packages everywhere. 'Okay,
enough of food. Now parcels. Let's see. This is the good
part.'

'What on earth…?'

He wasn't listening. 'What's in here?' He stared down
at the box and then grinned again. 'Oh, I know. I've lived
for long enough without my computer. I bought a new lap-
top this afternoon. Mine was due for an upgrade anyway.
I organized a service provider while I was in town, so it's
all systems go. All I need is a phone line and the internet
is at our disposal.'

As if on cue, Toby woke up and squawked. The internet
might be waiting, but so was Toby!

'He can't be hungry,' Rose said, staring at the computer
in fascination before crossing to look helplessly down at
her son. 'It's only two hours.'

'He doesn't need food. He needs information,' Tom said
sagely. He scooped Toby out of his crib and set him on his
knee. 'I'll bet he'll take to computers like a fish to water.
Okay, young Toby. Let's introduce you to your world. How
about seeing if we can find out all we need to know about
bloodhounds on the internet?'

If anyone had told Rose two weeks ago that she'd be spending this evening with a strange man, sorting through information on the internet while her tiny son lay on his knee,
she'd have thought they were crazy. But that was exactly
what she was doing. She took Toby from Tom but in the
end she was laughing so much she had to give him back.

Bloodhounds…

'They're not as easy to train as farm dogs,' Tom pronounced gravely, having found at least thirty interesting

sites. 'Actually—' his nose screwed up '—this looks a bit disgusting.'

'It says they drool,' Rose said, staring at the screen and then turning to stare down at Yoghurt. 'Surely not.'

'According to this, if they aim right when they shake their heads, then their drool can reach the ceiling,' Tom added. 'And it dries so hard that it's been given as an option to NASA for sticking its tiles onto space shuttles.'

'Yoghurt doesn't drool!'

'Maybe she only drools when she's happy. It says here that a happy bloodhound can clear a coffee table with one swipe of her tail. Yoghurt's tail goes back and forth about ten inches—and that's when she's really, really excited.'

'Like now,' Rose said slowly, watching her. 'You'd think a bloodhound would be excited at rump steak.'

'She is.'

'But not as excited as any of these hounds. Maybe we have a depressed bloodhound.'

'Maybe she's having her five minutes of post-natal depression—multiplied by seven.'

'Maybe she was depressed when we got her.'

We… The *we* slipped out unconsciously and, as Rose realized she'd said it, she flashed an uncertain glance at Tom.

It hadn't registered.

Of course it hadn't. We… It sounded right to Tom. Perfectly natural.

'Maybe if we give her rump steak every day she'll cheer up,' Tom said.

'Yeah, right. In your dreams. You may be made of cash but there's no way I can afford—'

'I'm paying, Rose,' Tom said harshly. 'Let's get one thing straight. I lumbered you with Yoghurt, and if you keep her then I'll continue paying for her. There's no way

I'm walking away leaving you with any more responsibilities.'

'She's not a responsibility. You said yourself we could train her as a farm dog.'

Damn, she'd said *we* again. She had to stop.

But once again he hadn't noticed. 'Maybe not,' he said glumly, staring at the screen. 'It says here that these dogs are so dumb they trail scents without seeing anything else. It says that if you let them loose and they're following a scent they'll walk into parked cars, the odd tree or two…moving cars! It says a loose bloodhound is a dead bloodhound.'

'Don't listen, Yoghurt,' Rose said, startled. Yoghurt wolfed down her last mouthful of steak, looked enquiringly up at them and then lumbered over to lay her big head on Rose's lap. 'You'll be very useful, won't you, darling? For…for tracking lost cows.'

'You do have fences,' Tom said dryly. 'How many lost cows do you have in a year?'

'In the fog…'

'How often do we have fog?'

We… He was saying it himself now.

'Once or—or twice a year.'

'And we have eight bloodhounds. Boy, are we prepared! Maybe keeping them isn't such a good idea.'

'I don't know what else we can do.' She sighed. 'Maybe we'll be able to sell the puppies.'

'Do people buy moles?'

'They'll be really cute,' Rose said doubtfully, looking down at the blind litter of puppies. I think…'

'Seriously…'

'Seriously, let's not worry about it,' Rose said firmly. 'The bloodhounds stay!'

That made it easier, he didn't think! Tom stared at Rose

while she fondled the big dog's ears. To walk away from Rose and two babies—and Yoghurt and seven puppies...

What else could he do? He looked down at Toby lying on his lap and the baby looked up at him, eyes wide and trusting.

To walk away...

Good grief, what was the alternative?

'Joan said you sent her some money,' he said softly, watching her face as he changed tack. 'After Chris died.'

'When I sold the furniture I paid off what I could from the debts,' she said. 'And anything that comes in from the farm I'll use to pay them back.'

'What, all Chris's debts?'

'The ones he took on after we were married. The ones people were loaded with because of me—because they trusted my name so they didn't ask the questions they should have.'

'You'll be poverty-stricken for life!'

She tilted her chin. 'Better than being in debt. And we still have the farm.'

'You mean the children still have the farm. You have a lifetime of hard work to keep it for them.'

'I don't mind.'

'Well, I do.'

He glowered and she tried to glower back. It didn't quite come off. Instead, she lifted Toby away from him and cuddled him close.

'I—it's getting close to feed time.'

Tom looked at her in silence for a moment and then took the hint. Okay. If she didn't want to talk about it then he wouldn't make her. He cheered up. 'Okay, if it's feed time then it's bathtime, too. Which makes it time for my next conjuring trick.'

'Conjuring...'

'I've bought baby gifts,' he said proudly. 'My first ever

baby gifts. Tell me what you think.' He took Toby back
from her and carried him over to a pile of parcels by the
door. 'Come on, Toby. It's present time. Let's wake up that
big sister of yours and see what Uncle Tom has brought
you.'

Uncle Tom had been thoroughly, totally ridiculous. He'd
bought so much it was enough to cause an economic upturn
in the district all by itself. Rose sat on the floor, surrounded
by babies and a sea of tissue paper, and gazed around,
stunned.

He'd bought two of everything. Two teddies. Two spin-
ning tops. Two rattles. And two night-lights with stars and
moons floating around in a gentle misty sea.

There were two baby carriers complete with bedding.
'Set up for the truck when it's mended,' Tom said seriously.
'So you can take them for afternoon drives, or with you
down to the paddocks when you're checking the cattle.'

'Tom.'

'And look at this.' He opened his next gift with the air
of a genie conjuring things from thin air. Out tumbled a
pile of baby clothes that made Rose gasp.

There'd be no more need for the horrid yellow jogging
suits. Here were soft pink and blue matinée jackets and soft,
soft rompers. Tiny bootees. Little vests and gorgeous cash-
mere shawls. Everything the best dressed baby about town
could possibly desire.

Here was everything Rose could ever dream of giving to
her children.

Tom laid the babies down on a shawl apiece and looked
anxiously at their mother. 'Well?'

She didn't answer. She couldn't. She lifted up one thing
after another, staring sightlessly at his gifts. The silence
stretched out for ever.

'You don't like them?' Tom demanded.

'I—' She sniffed desperately and searched for a handkerchief. Then she blew her nose and looked at him wildly over the cloth. 'I do, but...'

'Rose...'

He moved then, across the litter of tissue paper and toys and clothing, and hauled her to him, hugging her close. She melted into him, handkerchief still pressed against her face, but now it was also pressed against his chest and the sound of her valiant sniffs made him smile. She didn't cry...

She was some lady!

'Rose.' He'd never held a woman like this. He'd never felt about a woman like this! He cradled her to him while she fought desperately for control, and he felt an overwhelming desire to hold her exactly where she was. For ever...

Which was crazy. He was a man who craved adventure, whose job it was to move on. He told himself that over and over as he held her close. And even closer...

Finally she pulled herself together. He found another handkerchief deep in his trouser pocket—hey, it must have been there for months—and handed it to her with due solemnity. Then he held her at arm's length while she blew her nose. Twice.

She looked down at the cloth and managed a chuckle. 'You want it back?'

'I'll bury it,' he said magnanimously. 'My spadework's getting better and better.'

She chuckled, a lovely throaty chuckle, laced with tears. 'Oh, Tom.'

That got to him. Her saying his name. Heaven knows why it should but it made his heart twist.

'Rose.'

'I can't keep all this,' she managed, looking up at him. He was still holding her; his hands grasped her shoulders and their eyes were locked. 'You must see that I can't.'

'Why not?'

'You're a stranger!'

'No, I'm not,' he said, wounded. 'I'm Tom!'

He was too, she thought mistily. Her wonderful Tom. Her genie with his magic lamp who made things better…

But this was the real world. Not a fairy story.

Somehow she collected herself together, out of his reach. The babies were free from their wrapping and were lying on their backs in the pile of gifts, seemingly content to feel these new sensations, and to check out the sights and sounds around them. A whole new world was wakening for them.

But not for Rose. Somehow Rose had to remember that it was the same old world—a world where reality hurt.

'If you knew how much I've wanted to buy all this,' she whispered, looking around her at the lovely gifts. 'I'm just the same as every mother, I guess. I want my children to have everything. The best. But I can't. They can't.'

'I've just given it to them, Rose,' Tom told her, his eyes on her face. 'You can't give it back. It's my gift to them.'

Her chin tilted. 'I can give it back. I must.'

'Why?'

'I'm beholden to you enough already.'

'I hit your car, remember,' Tom said softly. 'I made your babies come early.'

'I did have pains before you hit me,' she told him. 'You're not to feel guilty. And you don't—' she met his look, defiant '—you don't feel guilty, do you?'

No. He didn't. It was true, he hadn't hurt her, and if he hadn't hit her truck and she'd gone on home alone she might have had to deliver the twins herself.

No, he didn't feel guilty, but he still felt bound, and he didn't know what was doing the binding.

'How do you think I'd feel,' she demanded, lifting a shawl and fingering its softness, 'carrying my babies around the district dressed better than most around here can afford? When I owe everyone so much.'

'You don't owe. They're Chris's debts. Joan will make sure everyone knows it.'

'They're my debts. They were incurred because of me. People trusted Chris because he was married to me.'

'So you'll punish the children.' That wasn't fair and he knew it. He watched the pain wash over her face and he hated himself for saying it, but, damn, she had to accept. 'You'll deprive them of my gifts.'

'They'll live,' she said drearily.

They would. Tom looked at her for a long, long moment. She was so beautiful, sitting there in her faded jeans and her loose man's shirt with the top three buttons perennially undone for feeding. Her face was still pale from long months of worry and exhaustion, her curls tousled and un-kempt, and yet her chin was set with stubborn determina-tion.

Yes, they'd live—without him.

'Rose, I really need to give you these gifts,' he said softly, trying to make her see. 'I have more than enough money to afford it.'

That was certainly true. The lifestyle he led was high-risk, but the rewards were fabulous, and he didn't spend money. He invested it all. He could retire now and he'd be rich.

'You don't need to give me anything,' she said stub-bornly.

'I can't walk away and leave you in poverty.'

She shook her head, her eyes clear and direct. She knew what she must do—what she must say—even though it hurt like a knife in her heart. 'Tom, you're nothing to do with us. Nothing. You've been wonderful. You're a truly amaz-ing person, and you've given us so much. All of us. Me and the twins and Yoghurt. You've given us all a new life.

But now—you've given enough.' She took a deep breath. 'Maybe it's time for you to move on.'

Move on…

The words seemed to echo round and round the big room. Toby was lying against the tissue paper and it crinkled as he moved. It was the only sound…

Tom looked across at Rose and he felt his gut twist in pain. To move on…

But she was right. There was nothing he could give her that was useful. Nothing.

Except…

The thought came from nowhere, blinding in its simplicity. Of course. There was one thing he had—and it was of no use to anyone else. Maybe…maybe it could work.

Jessie whimpered beside him and he lifted her automatically and held her close. 'Hush,' he told her. 'Hush for a minute. There's something I want to ask your mum.'

'What?' Rose said drearily, starting to collect tissue paper and fold it into neat little squares. Anything so she didn't have to look at him.

'Put that down, Rose.'

'Why?'

'I've just had a brilliant idea.' He smiled, his eyes trying to tease her out of her misery. 'Well, I could say that, wouldn't I? All my ideas are brilliant. But this one takes the cake.'

'What is it?' She was still on automatic pilot but she had ceased folding her paper to look at him. That was a mistake! Those eyes were almost magnetic.

He hesitated, and the twinkle in his eyes faded.

She frowned. 'Tom?'

'Tell me if I'm being stupid,' he said softly, 'but I think…maybe for both of us it could work.'

'What could work?'

'How would you feel,' he said slowly, thinking it over in his mind as he spoke, 'how would you feel about marrying me?'

CHAPTER SIX

How would you feel about marrying me...?

The words hung in the air like the hovering of an up-raised sword, threatening to crash down on them, slashing all before it. That was just how Rose looked, Tom thought as he watched her face—as if something dreadful was about to come smashing down on her. But he couldn't take back the words.

'Hey, Rose, I'm not talking about doom, defeat or despair here,' he said hurriedly, reaching out to touch her hand. 'It's only marriage.'

She pulled back as if his fingers burned. 'Only marriage? What sort of a joke is that?'

'It's no joke, Rose.'

'It must be.' She took a deep breath. 'Marriage. I've only known you for six days. I don't know the first thing about you.'

He smiled, his eyes watchful. 'What do you want to know? I'm thirty-three and I've never been married. I'm a normal heterosexual guy with no known deviations. I change my socks every day, I like beer, I don't snore and I won't eat spinach if you pay me. Oh, and I've learned nappy-changing and spade-handling in just six days. I'm a fast learner. What else is there to know?'

That brought a smile to her face, but it didn't last long. It faded almost as it reached her eyes. 'You know I didn't mean...things like that.'

'What else do you need to know?'

'Things like... ' she took a deep breath '...like why on

earth a sane, sensible man would pick someone like me and ask them to marry them.'

Someone like me. She really did think like that, Tom saw. Chris had made her self-worth plummet to an all-time low. He'd married her to get her farm, and she knew it. *Someone like me* meaning someone less than worthless...

'Why wouldn't I want to marry you?' he asked softly.

'Well, for a start, you don't know *me*.'

'I do.' His jaw turned stubborn on that one because it was so easy to answer. 'I've seen you at your most distressed, your most vulnerable. You have raw courage, Rose, and you're the most beautiful woman...'

'You're not pretending you've fallen in love with me?'

That was harder. Tom's brow furrowed. Love?

No. He didn't think so. Love was something he wasn't capable of giving. Yeah, sure, he was a normal guy, but he'd been kicked in the guts too often to think he could ever fall in love.

'Maybe not.'

'Then why on earth are you thinking of marriage?'

Good question. He hardly knew himself.

It was just as well the twins were quiet. He needed time to think this through.

She gave him time. Rose's eyes were on his face but she didn't push him.

'You need to be married,' he said at last, and her eyes widened.

'If that's the only reason then it's plain stupid. I'm not some charity.'

'No, but...' It was hard, sorting out the jumble of emotions in his head. He wasn't used to emotion. He was used to hard-headed plans, and that was what he needed now.

'It could suit us both,' he told her at last, his voice leveling as his brain went into organisational mode. He lined up his arguments in his head, but then, as he was about to start, Jess decided she was fed up with gifts and wanted food. Reminded of the important things in life, Toby roared in agreement.

Tom groaned with a mixture of resignation and relief. 'We'll talk after feeding.'

'But—'

'Let me think things out properly before we talk,' he told her, lifting her son and carrying both babies towards the bath. 'I want to get this right.'

She looked sideways at him—rather as if he'd just grown another head but she wasn't game enough to point it out in case he took it personally—and then seemed to acquiesce.

There was little else to do with a nut case.

He wasn't a nut case. The next half-hour was taken up with bathing and feeding, and when peace finally reigned Tom had it worked out. His plan was sane and sensible, and totally logical. But first he had to set the scene.

'Hot chocolate,' he told her as she straightened from settling her twin. 'And a Tim Tam.'

'Tim Tam?'

'They're the only reason I keep coming back to Australia,' he told her, ripping open the biscuit packet and munching into his Tim Tam with relish. 'That and to see my mother,' he added hurriedly. 'Rose, sit. Let's leave clearing the bath stuff till later.'

She sat and eyed him with caution. 'You're not going to start up this crazy idea of marriage again?'

'You're looking at me like I'm a sandwich short of a picnic.'

'A kangaroo loose in the top paddock,' she agreed placidly, keeping things low-key. 'Nuts.'

'But nice nuts?' he asked hopefully, and she had to smile.

'Definitely nice nuts. But, Tom, this marriage idea… Just leave it because it really is stupid. It'll spoil…' Her voice faltered.

'Spoil what?'

'Spoil this little time.' She lifted a Tim Tam from the packet and bit into it, but she hardly saw what she was eating. It was a waste of a perfectly good Tim Tam, he thought humorously, and removed the packet from her reach.

'Don't!'

'Don't what?'

'Eat your Tim Tam without due reverence. I'll show you how you should do it.' He extracted another biscuit from the packet and bit off its chocolatey ends. He dipped one bitten end in his hot chocolate, then sucked the hot chocolate up through the biscuit.

The look on his face was orgasm territory and Rose couldn't resist. She burst into her delicious chuckle and Tom licked his chocolatey lips and grinned.

'You try.'

'No. I—'

He handed her another Tim Tam. 'I insist. Absolutely. I've bought twenty packets of these things so there's plenty to practise on.'

'Twenty packets!' The look she gave him told him he'd just sprouted a *third* head—but she bit her Tim Tam and slurped.

Good grief!

'It's gorgeous, isn't it?' Tom demanded as she finally surfaced.

'I— yes.' It was the only thing she could think of to say. She was so close to laughter. So close to tears.

From marriage to Tim Tams—he lurched from the crazy to the ridiculous!

But Tom was taking her mug of chocolate and placing

it on the table. 'There you are, then. Life's full of good
things, Rose,' he said gently, and he reached forward and
took her hands in his. 'If you're prepared to take the
chance. To try.'

'I am.'

'You're not. Or maybe you were but you've forgotten
how, and I don't see how you can find out again, living
like this.'

'I don't see why…'

'Rose, you're nearly out of cattle feed,' he said conversationally, ignoring her interruption. 'Joan tells me you
didn't harvest all your hay and everyone wondered why
not.'

'I was pregnant and alone. I couldn't harvest it all by
myself and I couldn't afford to employ someone to do it
for me.'

'I know that,' he said gently, and the linking of their
hands was absolute. He hardly had to speak. It was as if
she knew what he'd say before he opened his mouth. 'But
there's two more months before you can expect enough
new spring growth. How will you feed? You'll have to sell
some stock to afford to feed the rest.'

'Yes, but—'

'And then how will you restock? What's your income
going to be?'

'I guess—' she bit her lip '—when the feed goes, I'll
have to sell the cattle and lease the farm. Move into town.'

'And come back when?'

'When the twins are older.'

'You mean when the twins are adult,' he said ruthlessly.
Still he held her hands and she appeared not to notice. In
fact, the feel of his hands was good. It was warm and com-
forting, even though what he was saying was the cold, un-
palatable truth. 'Rose, you'll have to pay to rent a place in

town, your creditors are still waiting to take any cent you earn—and you love this farm.'

'I know, but—'

'Marry me and I'll pay to keep you on it.'

That startled her enough to pull away—but he wasn't having a bar of it. His grip tightened. 'Listen, Rose,' he said strongly. 'I have more than enough to invest in this place and keep it running, and to do so would give me pleasure.'

'I told you,' she managed dully, pulling at her hands. 'I'm not a charity.'

'And I'm not making a donation. That's why I'm asking you if you'll marry me. I want something in return.'

'Like—what?'

'You.'

Her eyes flew to his face. 'Tom.'

'Oh, I'm not saying I've fallen in love here,' he said hastily, refusing even to let the possibility filter though his head. 'I'm not that sort of man. But it doesn't stop me wanting…'

He took a deep breath and looked around. The kitchen was warm and snug. The twins, fed to the Plimsoll line, were snoozing in their cribs. Yoghurt was sleeping by the fire, and her pups were suckling around her. The litter made by Tom's gifts was colourful chaos in the homely room. It was a wonderful place to be. 'I want this,' Tom said.

'What?'

He shrugged and released her hands to motion around the room. 'This. I've never had it.'

'I don't understand.'

'My mother wasn't a settling sort of person,' Tom said softly. 'She hauled me from relationship to relationship and I never had a chance to call anywhere home or to grow attached. Well, it's left me so I can't spend more than a

few weeks with a woman or in one place without wanting
out. But this…a home…'

'A home without strings?' she said slowly, and Tom
shrugged again.

'It sounds stupid but I've been thinking. Most of the guys
I meet on the oil rigs have wives back home. They send
off their pay cheque and they visit when they can. I shove
my pay cheque in the bank and then when I get leave I
have nowhere to go. Even five-star hotels start feeling the
same after a while. They're impersonal and cold
and…empty. So I sort of thought—'

'You'd like to put your boots under my bed when you're
on leave?' Rose asked, and if her voice sounded a bit harsh
she couldn't help it.

'That's not what I'm saying.' He grimaced. 'The sex
thing, Rose… well, if it happens…if after you've gotten
over the birth of the twins and you want it—if we both
want it—then well and good, but if not I'll live without it.'

She stared. 'Tom, exactly what sort of marriage are you
looking for?' she asked.

'I just want—' Hell, he'd been trying to sort it out in his
mind for the past hour and it still wasn't clear. 'I just want
the thought of this place. While I'm working.'

She frowned, her eyes concentrating on his. She was trying to see into his mind. Trying to see his need.

'You put out oil-well fires,' she said slowly. 'Right?'

'Right.'

'And something's happened…recently, I mean…to make
you feel like this?'

'No.'

'Yes,' she said softly. 'It has. There's trouble behind
your eyes, Tom Bradley, and I can see it as clearly as you
can see mine. What's made you want a wife and children
all of a sudden?'

'I don't want...' He paused and shrugged but she wasn't letting him off the hook that easily.

'What do you want?'

'I just want the thought of it,' he told her. 'I guess you're right. What I do is dangerous work. There's always the fumes—sulphur dioxide mixed with things like arsenic, lead and copper—and the fear of explosion. When you're working around fires where the temperature rises to four thousand degree temperatures and the sand gets so hot it turns to molten glass, there's always the risk of disaster.'

'Oh, great,' she said faintly. 'Nappy-changing pales in comparison.'

'Don't you believe it,' he said darkly, and she grinned. But her smile died almost as soon as it appeared.

'So what happened?'

'I don't...'

'If you don't tell me, then we take this conversation no further,' she told him. 'I'm off to bed. And—' she glowered '—I'll take the Tim Tams with me.'

'No, ma'am,' he said in mock horror. 'Not the Tim Tams!'

Her smile faded again. 'Tell me what's happened to cause the pain behind your eyes.'

Tom flinched. She saw—she saw too darn much!

'You don't want to hear,' he started harshly, but this time her hands gripped his, not the other way around.

'Tom! Tell me!'

He was trapped. Hell!

For a long minute he was silent, and she thought he wouldn't speak. His gaze fell away from her eyes and rested on their linked hands. Hers were so much smaller than his—finer but work-worn. Calloused... She'd worked too hard for a woman...

A muscle worked at the corner of his mouth, the only outward sign of an inner struggle.

'Tom?' she said softly.

And he told her. Sort of…

'It was my best mate,' he said heavily. 'Marty Helder. We'd worked together for years. They used to call us The Invincible Pair, and among hell-fighters that's quite a reputation.'

'Hell-fighters?'

'What they call oil-well-fire experts.'

'Oh,' she said faintly. She swallowed. 'So…what happened to Marty?'

'Just…' He looked up at her face and what he read there threatened to undo him. He'd been so in control up to now. Right from the point where he'd sealed off the area where Marty lay. He'd known Marty was dead. There was no way anyone could be alive in that inferno. But to seal it off and walk away—and then wait for the explosion.

Dear God… He couldn't go on.

But he didn't need to go any further. 'Don't say it, then,' Rose said softly and she reached up and touched his face. 'I can see it. You don't have to tell me any more.' She ran her fingers down, tracing his cheekbone, and a shudder ran right through his body.

No. He didn't need to tell her. He already had. He looked up and met her luminous gaze and he knew that she spoke the truth. She saw the horror. She saw what he couldn't speak of without breaking down.

'Marty was like me,' he said at last. 'No ties. It was just as well there was nothing to find at the end, because there was no one to bury him but me, and the fortune Marty has earned will go to some cousin he's never set eyes on.' He took a deep breath.

'I'd like mine to go to you, and the twins. Even to Yoghurt!'

'If that's what this is about…' she said, startled. 'Signing

off so we can inherit when you turn into a human barbe-
cue…'

'Hey, I didn't mean that.'

'What did you mean?'

'It'd just be good,' he told her slowly, still working it
out in his head, 'to know you were here. To know my pay
cheque was going somewhere and that I was working for
something.'

'For a home.'

'It wouldn't be my home,' he told her, and his voice was
harsh again. 'I don't have a home. As I said, I don't settle.
But I could visit—spend a few weeks each year feeding
cows and changing nappies and throwing balls for dogs…'

His voice was so wistful that Rose stared. 'Tom, if that's
what you really want…'

'I don't,' he said abruptly. 'At least not for good. I never
have wanted something like that for keeps. Just every now
and then.' He pulled away and rose, crossing the room to
stand and stare sightlessly out of the darkened window. His
back was stiff and unyielding and Rose knew that the tension in him was rising to breaking point.

She sighed and went over to touch him lightly on the
shoulder. Her touch made him flinch. He didn't understand
himself what he was fighting, she thought, and wondered
whether she did.

'Leave it, Tom,' she said softly. 'It's late and you're
tired. We'll talk about it in the morning. Let's go to bed.'

'I need to check the cows.'

'I'll check them.'

'But…'

'We have a truck now,' she reminded him. 'It'll only
take me twenty minutes to go around the paddocks in the
hire truck and I'd really like to get out. It'll be the first
time since the twins were born, and I'd like to see how my

girls are doing. You stay here and mind the twins. And Yoghurt and the pups. Your nine babies.'

'Rose.'

'Domesticity's not half bad,' she told him. 'Just keep on trying it, Tom Bradley. Or at least try it for twenty minutes while I clear my head.'

There were no cows stuck in the mud tonight, for which Rose was profoundly grateful. She didn't want to fetch Tom for a bit of digging, and she was still in no state to be digging herself.

She drove around the first water-hole, checked the second, and then parked the truck and stared out over the moonlit water.

She was so confused she hardly knew where she was.

Marriage.

Tom.

The two were so interwoven in her mind that they were a tangled mesh, refusing to be separated. Marriage to Tom…

Marriage? No!

But Tom…

What had he called himself? A hell-fighter. A man who went from trouble spot to trouble spot, seeking out danger. One who wanted marriage as a balm to his soul because he knew he could die at any time.

He was hardly husband material.

But…Tom?

Tom himself was husband material in full. She only had to think of him to smile—his lovely big body, weathered and tough as nails, and his huge hands, cradling her babies as if they were the most precious things in the world.

His gorgeous smile and his kindness…

It was enough to be the undoing of any woman, she

thought in confusion, let alone one whose hormones were leaping all over the place due to childbirth. At least that must be why they were leaping about. That must be the reason. Wasn't it?

Or were they leaping at the thought of marriage...?

Of Tom.

Somehow she had to make herself think past the thought of his face—the thought of what Tom as a husband could be....

Focus!

What was he asking? That she marry him and keep the home fires burning—with no strings attached. That she be some kind of non-wife.

She was never going to be any other kind, she told herself bleakly. Riddled with debt, with two tiny children to support—saddled with the emotional baggage from Chris.

No. He was right when he guessed there was no way she'd contemplate another marriage.

But with Tom...

Maybe it could work.

No!

Why not? she asked herself, and found the answer staring her in the face. It was so obvious it was blinding. She knew why she couldn't marry him and it wasn't because the idea was crazy.

She couldn't marry him because he'd leave her. He'd head off into the big bad world and fight his fires and she'd never know whether he was dead or alive.

I'd go nuts, she told herself. And there's no way I can make a decision like this the week my babies are born. No way!

She sighed and started the truck, turning it towards home. As she did she caught sight of something at the edge of her vision. A cow was down on the far side of the paddock.

Why? Calving wasn't due to start for months yet. Rose frowned, but headed over to see.

It was a heifer, a small animal that Rose had kept separate. She was too small to calf this year, but that was just what she was doing—or trying to do.

'Oh, no.' Rose pulled to a halt and clambered out of the truck, bending over the cow to see. What she saw in the brightness of the headlights made her flinch.

'That damned bull.'

She knew what had happened. It was her fences—or, rather, lack of them. The bull had got out one afternoon. When she'd found him, Ferdinand the Bull was standing nonchalantly by the break in the fence, as if he'd just got through. As if butter wouldn't melt in his mouth—the picture of innocence.

But he'd obviously been busy before she reached him.

'He must have guessed you were one of the girls not included in his harem this year,' Rose said in distress. 'And I didn't notice you were pregnant. I've been too focussed on me. Oh, girl, I'm sorry.'

She put her hand on the cow's flank, and felt it heave. The cow rolled her eyes in panic.

How long had she been down? It must have been a while by the look of the churned land around her.

'I'll have to go back and get the calving chains,' Rose said, pushing herself to her feet and grimacing. She was still sore from birthing herself. 'Hold on, girl. I'll be right back.'

'And where do you think you might be going?'

Rose jumped a foot in the air. She was reaching into the back of her old truck to get what she needed and she hadn't heard Tom come up behind her. Now his hand landed on her shoulder and she yelped.

'Do you mind?' she quavered. 'You just about gave me a palsy stroke.'

'What's a palsy stroke?'

'I have no idea,' she snapped. 'But I nearly found out.'

'So what are we doing?'

'*I*,' she said fiercely, 'am getting the calving chains.'

'We're doing a spot of calving?'

'I.'

'We.' He lifted the chains from her grasp and fixed her with a look. 'You're not lifting anything heavier than a baby.'

'He didn't mean that.'

'If the doctor didn't mean it, then he wouldn't have said it. He did—and so do I. You're lifting nothing. Tell me where the cow is, Rose.'

'You're not doing it yourself. You won't have a clue what to do.'

'Hey, I've delivered twins,' he said in mock indignation. 'And septuplets. How many obstetricians do you know who can say that? A single calf should be a pushover.'

'She's in trouble, Tom,' Rose said, pushing her curls back from her tired face. 'She's too young to calf and the calf will be a big one.'

'So tell me what to do.'

'I can't. I'll have to do it.'

'No!'

'But I must.'

'Then come with me and show me what to do.'

She cast an uncertain glance at the house. 'But—the twins.'

'That's what I bought the baby carriers for,' he said proudly. 'For transport. So let's collect what we need, and then you and I and Jessie and Toby will ride to the rescue. Hell-fighter style.'

'Tom…'

'We're wasting time, Rose,' he said gently. 'Let's go.'

* * *

It was a long and tedious birth, and anyone without Tom's patience would have given up and put the cow out of its misery. But Tom wasn't having a bar of it. If Rose knew what to do, then he was behind her every step of the way.

They took soap and water down, lubricated everything in sight, attached the calving chains and then sat and waited. As each contraction passed, Tom put all his weight behind the chains—something Rose could never have done. She sat on the grass next to him, a twin sleeping peacefully in each of the carriers beside her, and gave directions.

And watched Tom.

But Tom was intent only on the task at hand. The cow was so small—and the calf was so big.

'Can't we call the vet?' Tom asked as he saw the trouble the cow was in, but Rose shook her head.

'I paid him but I asked Chris to post the cheques. He didn't, so I still owe him. I haven't managed to clear my debt. He won't come.'

'So it's down to us.'

'It's down to us.'

Tom put his hand on the cow's flank and ran it along her smooth hide.

'Don't you worry, girl. Just take your time. We're all behind you, every step of the way.'

He moved to get behind his chains again, and Rose suddenly felt her throat constrict in a surge of emotion so real she could taste it.

We're all behind you…

She'd been so alone, and now here was Tom.

He was asking for marriage.

Impossible. And yet, if she didn't say yes, he'd ride off to his hell-fires and she'd never see him again. Or maybe he'd end up as a statistic… Three killed in the oil fires in

Kuwait…seventy-three expats killed abroad this year…
deaths by accident, one thousand four hundred and twenty-
six…

'It's moving!' Tom's voice cut across her morbid fan-
cies—of Tom trapped by fire, Tom's flag-draped coffin being brought home, Tom being lowered into an open grave.
Suddenly, blessedly, it was the real Tom she was looking
at, and he was very much alive, his shirt-sleeves hitched
right up to his shoulders, his jeans grass-stained in the
moonlight and one of the knees ripped, his muscled arms
all brawn as he put every ounce of power he had behind
the chains. His strongly boned face was absolutely intent
on the task at hand—the life of a calf.

And then a massive contraction ripped through the poor
little cow, Tom's arms tightened and whitened with strain,
and all of a sudden the tiny calf lost its resistance. It slipped
out in a rush, leaving Tom sprawled backwards on the
grass.

The calf was alive! Rose gave a whoop of pure delight
and knelt forward to clear its airway, but Tom was before
her.

'Hey, no! This is my job. I'm the obstetrician,' he said
proudly, and he lifted the perfect heifer calf and carried her
so that her exhausted mum could nose her gently and claim
her as her own.

He was *so* pleased.

Rose sat back in the moonlight and looked at the picture
before her. Her smallest cow, recovering by the second,
nosing a healthy calf and giving it some first tentative
licks—and Tom beaming fit to burst.

Even if I can have this for only a week a year, she said
softly to herself, even if he dies and I'm not there…

She closed her eyes, and when she opened them she
knew what she would do. So when Tom came bouncing

over to where she sat, reached down and grabbed her in a hug of triumph she hugged him right back.

Only not a hug as he'd meant to be hugged. She wrapped her arms around his neck, held him close—closer—and she kissed him.

It was some kiss, and it was a kiss that changed things for ever. It wasn't a kiss of friendship. It was a kiss of pure proprietorship. Of claiming her own.

And there was a bit of lust thrown in for good measure.

As her lips met his, the kiss blasted through their consciousness, searing them with heat and power and an aching hunger that shook them both to the core.

And that scared them both stupid.

She wasn't ready for it. No! She couldn't—she couldn't give herself to a man like this. Open her heart…

But how could she help it? She held him to her and she felt her head fill with a brilliant joy—with light after shadow, with the promise of life to come.

And Tom?

He'd never felt like this. Her lips, her touch, her taste… The way her body curved to his.

Her very being.

When finally he put her away from him he gazed down at her with eyes that were dazed and shocked.

Hell! There was an agenda here that he hadn't planned— a linking that he didn't understand in the least. That scared him.

But she was smiling at him, placing her hands in his, giving him her trust and her promise, and it was far, far too late to draw back.

'Okay, Tom Bradley,' she whispered in a voice that was none too steady. 'Okay, my hell-fighter. My obstetrician *extraordinaire*…'

'Okay, what?' His voice wasn't all that steady either. The kiss had shaken a few things he'd never had before and he was finding it really, really hard not to haul her back into his arms and kiss her again. But he didn't want to. He *couldn't* want to.

'I'll marry you,' she said. 'Whatever you're prepared to give— it won't be enough, but if that's all there is—well, I'll marry you. Whenever you want. Just name your terms.'

CHAPTER SEVEN

IT TOOK four weeks to arrange the wedding and those four weeks saw Tom running through a gamut of emotions he'd never felt in his life before.

One part of him wanted to soak up every sweet part of this—to take his new family to him and love them as he'd never been able to love anything in his life.

The other part of him wanted to run a mile. Or half a world! That was the part of him that was scared silly.

Which was one crazy way to face a wedding, he thought on his wedding morning as he made his way down to the paddocks to check the cattle. Wedding or no wedding, the cows still needed feeding, and by now even getting out of the house was a relief. This place was starting to close in on him in a way that made his head feel as if it was bursting.

'You're a lucky man,' the neighbours told him, clapping him on the shoulder. 'She's a good lass, and you'll make a fine couple.'

Rose would make a fine half of any couple, he thought. But he—he didn't have what it took. Staying power. A marriage was supposed to be until death, only this marriage was until the next call came and he could be off, giving himself breathing time—an escape route—so that he wouldn't get too attached. So the twins and Rose wouldn't get attached to him, either. Too dependent. Because if they depended on him they'd be hurt!

This was stupid!

Yes, this was wrong, but that was the way he was born, he decided bitterly. Or maybe it was the way his mother had raised him to be. But there was no avoiding how he felt. Panic-stricken! As if the walls were closing in. His wedding suggestion had been crazy, and now he was committed to it and he didn't like the ramifications one bit.

The for ever part—the way everyone assumed it was for ever, and that he loved Rose, and that...

He did love Rose.

Not like that! Not wanting to be beside her fifty years from now. Or maybe—maybe he did want that, but he knew it wasn't going to happen and that was the thing that was scaring him!

So, get back to practicalities. When all else failed, get to work!

He dumped the hay bales off the truck, looking round the herd with satisfaction as he did. At least this was working. Things looked good here. The herd had picked up in the last four weeks on the good feed he'd brought in. His special little cow, still with her calf at her feet, was almost as big as the rest of the herd now. Next time he came home he'd be lucky if he could tell her apart.

Next time he came *home*.

It wouldn't be for a long, long while, he told himself, and his panic eased at the thought of an enforced absence. A few decent fires. Action! He could get away from here, cut his emotional ties, stop feeling so threatened, so closed in.

'I don't need this place,' he told his special cow as he tossed her her very own piece of hay bale. 'And I've done all I can.'

He had. The fences were mended or renewed. The track in from the road had been freshly levelled. He'd started painting the house and it looked a million dollars better for it.

There was a low woof near the truck and he looked down to see Yoghurt standing placidly by its back, waiting for a

heave-up. She'd taken to following him down to the paddock, taking time out from domestic duties. Her pups were
five weeks old now, and enough to try any mother's patience.

'You'll have to follow Sam when I'm away,' he told her,
hauling her droopy form up to join him on the tray. Sam
Baxter was the man he'd hired after interviewing more than
a dozen men. It had been hard to find someone he'd trust
to take care of the place while he was away, but Sam was
in his fifties, lean and weathered from a life of farming,
and more than capable of taking charge.

Except for nappy-changing, Tom thought darkly. Rose
was on her own for that, and he didn't like the thought.

'She'll manage without me,' Tom said grimly to
Yoghurt. 'She must. Because if I stay here much longer I'll
go nuts. Or I'll start running and not be able to stop.'

'Rose, you look just lovely.'

Joan Mitchell adjusted the tiny thread of rosebuds
she'd woven through Rose's curls, and then stood back to
see the effect. Her eyes misted with tears. 'Oh, my dear.
Your mother would be so proud.'

'Maybe my mother would say I'm being sensible at last,'
Rose told her, smoothing down the soft silk dress Tom had
bought her. It was palest apricot—Tom's only concession
to her widowhood—but 'if I'm going to be married I want
a bride', he'd said, and Rose had acquiesced.

She couldn't figure Tom out. Some days he didn't want
anything to do with the wedding, and then some days he
seemed so enthusiastic, wanting everything to be perfect—
his dream.

Which was just what it seemed to him, she thought sadly.
A dream. She and the twins would be the family Tom had
dreamed of but knew he could never have. Not really have.

She fingered her gorgeous dress, a tinge of guilt and sadness washing across her face. In truth, she loved this dress, even though the thought of what it had cost Tom gave her a pang.

It couldn't matter. Tom was pouring money into this place—into her life and into her children's lives—and she couldn't deny he was enjoying doing it.

'I want a list of your creditors,' he'd growled, and when she'd demurred he'd fixed her with a look. 'There's no way my wife's living in debt. What else is my money for if not to support my family?'

Which was all very well, but—family?

They weren't, Rose thought sadly. She had watched the panic in Tom's eyes every time she got close. He liked saying it, he liked feeling it, but no more than that. He let her only so near and no further.

And as for sex... Their kiss on the night he'd asked her to marry him had been the only time she'd been able to get near him. Every time she touched him now he backed off, and sometimes she had only to smile at him across a room and she could see the panic start behind his eyes.

He was being considerate because she needed time to get over the birth of the twins, she told herself—he was afraid of hurting her—but in her heart she knew it was more than that.

This was his legacy from his rotten childhood. Fear. He'd given his heart once too often to the 'families' his mother had landed him with, and he'd been hurt too often when she'd pulled him away again. That much Rose had been able to glean, but as for being able to do anything about it...

'He's so nice,' Joan breathed, seeing the trouble in her face and not understanding. 'Oh, Rose, with Tom I just know you won't have to worry about things like—I mean—'

'You mean he's not like Chris?'

'No,' Joan said bluntly. 'My Bob's had a good long talk to him and, apart from that dangerous job he does, he says he's a sensible man.'

No greater accolade could be given, Rose thought wryly, but the smile she gave was perfunctory.

Sensible...

Yes, he was sensible. He was doing the sensible thing, the honourable thing.

She looked out of the window and saw the truck weaving up through the cattle towards the house, Yoghurt wobbling gamely on the back.

Here he came. Her about-to-be husband. Her Tom.

Her love.

Her love who'd run a mile if he thought she loved him, she reminded herself, fingering the lovely stuff of her bridal gown. Her love who wanted to be anything but!

It was a mixed ceremony. First there was the small matter of naming two babies—because it seemed a shame to waste the vicar when he was coming specially, as Rose had said, and Tom had agreed.

So he stood to one side while Rose named her children.

Jessica Margaret Allen.

Tobias Thomas Allen.

His eyes widened at that. Thomas. He flashed a quizzical look at Rose but she smiled serenely back. Their nearest neighbours were here—twenty or so people who Tom knew could now be depended on to take care of Rose while he was away. They stood back and smiled happily at this naming ceremony, so Tom couldn't very well put in his oar and shout, Hey, I didn't want him named Thomas!

Thomas...Tobias Thomas.

There were papers Rose had given him to sign as well—

'Because if you're to be my husband then you need to go all the way.'

Adoption papers. It'd take two or three months before the adoption became legal but maybe, maybe in time Tobias Thomas Allen could be Tobias Thomas Bradley.

The old panic welled up in him again, and it was all he could do not to bolt for cover. But the vicar, Father Hendrick, was beaming and Joan was stepping forward to take two gurgling babies from their mother's arms so that the wedding could begin.

And then Rose was taking his hand—had he really stepped forward?—and the vicar moved so that he was addressing the pair of them.

They looked wonderful, the vicar thought as he prepared to marry them. They were a couple who were right for each other. She was beautiful—glowing, though a little unsure, more befitting a first-time bride than a widow. But her young man Tom Bradley in a dinner suit was a sight to behold. Handsome as could be. He was a fine young man, Father Hendrick had decided in the pre-marriage talks he'd had with the couple. They were making a wonderful home for these two babes, and only blessings could come from this match.

He had no qualms at all as he started to speak.

'Dearly beloved, we are gathered together here in the sight of God, and in the face of this congregation, to join this man and this woman...'

Rose touched Tom's hand lightly with hers, and the look she gave him was grave and questioning. He could still back out now, her look said, if he was unsure.

Dear heaven, could he? He looked down at her and all he saw was her loveliness.

I'm doing this for Rose, he told himself fiercely, looking away from her and back to the vicar. For Rose and the children. To keep them safe. This has nothing to do with me—with what I want. I'm still independent. I haven't given up anything that can hurt—if it's rejected again.

But… 'With this ring I thee wed,' Rose whispered, 'with my body I thee worship. All my worldly goods with thee I share.'

The world stood still. Tom stood frozen as the vicar went on with the wedding ceremony.

With my body I thee worship.

He knew truth when he heard it, and he heard it now. He looked down into her eyes and he saw truth there as well.

Tom might have organised a marriage of convenience—but she was playing for keeps.

It was a fine party as parties went. One humdinger of a wedding. District weddings were few and far between, and the locals weren't being denied their chance to celebrate in style.

Bob had brought his fiddle, Marg from down the road brought her keyboard, they set themselves up as a band and the guests danced until the daylight was a distant memory. The farm folk lapped it up. Rose hadn't wanted a formal reception, but the neighbours, guilt-ridden after their treatment of her, simply organised their own. There was food and to spare, dish after dish brought by every neighbour. This was a celebration to be proud of.

Even Yoghurt and her pups were in attendance. At five weeks old, the pups were roly-poly, bouncing bundles of mischief and Rose had done them up with a collar of rainbow-coloured ribbon apiece.

'Do you suppose they're leaving them on because they know it's an important occasion, or because they're stupid?' she'd asked, and Tom had grinned and scooped up an armful of beribboned pups.

'How can you say such a thing? Stupid? Don't listen, guys. I'll have no nasturtiums cast on your intelligence.'

They'd squirmed adoringly, trying to reach him with their long, wet tongues, and he'd set them down with a pang. He'd miss them when he left.

When he left...

He looked around the crowded room now. There was so much goodwill in this place, with his family and with his neighbours.

With his wife...

His wife in name, he told himself harshly. There was no way he was growing attached. He took a deep breath and grabbed Joan as she walked past with a plate of pavlova—and the next thing Joan knew she was being whirled crazily around the room, pavlova perilously aloft.

Keep on the move, he decided. That way he didn't have to think.

Finally, as midnight neared, Bob called for a hush.

'It's the bridal waltz,' he announced. 'One long dance for the bride and groom, ladies and gentlemen, and then we'll leave them to their new lives as a married couple.'

The applause sounded around them, every eye glistened with approval, and there was nothing else for it. Tom, who'd danced with nearly every woman but Rose, had to take his bride into his arms, against his heart.

She melted right into him. There was exhaustion showing in her lovely eyes. She'd had enough. The twins had woken her at five this morning, and she'd been on the move all day, making sure this day was perfect, and now she'd danced every dance...

'You should be in bed,' he told her as the bridal waltz started and he swung her easily out onto the floor. She fitted against his chest as if she belonged there, and her body moulded to his as if they were one.

'Will you take me there?' she whispered, and he started,

almost missing the beat. Surely he hadn't heard right? Or she hadn't meant…

He must concentrate on the dance.

How to concentrate on the dance when she felt so good, smelled so good, when her hands were on his waist and the heat was coursing though his body like an electric current?

But he didn't need to concentrate. The music was guide enough, and the beat in his head was the beat in his heart. They moved as one, and by the time the music drew to a close there wasn't a dry eye in the place.

A marriage made in heaven…

For a few more days, Tom told himself fiercely, desperately, and then it's over. I'll have a wife and family, but I'll be someplace else. I'll be on my own again.

Would you like coffee?'

Rose tucked in Toby after the final feed and turned to face her new husband. Jessie was already fed and fast asleep. Tom had been mechanically stacking glasses ready for the hire firm to collect tomorrow. He'd been waiting… Waiting for what?

'Leave those,' she told him gently. 'They can wait.'

'I'd rather do them tonight.' He didn't look at her. Every muscle, every nerve in his being was strained to breaking point. She was still in her lovely gown, the only concession to her domestic role being that she'd undone the tiny satin buttons at her breast. The result was incredibly—breathtakingly—seductive.

The rosebuds were still threaded in her hair. She'd slipped off her shoes and was padding around the room in bare feet. The sight of her naked toes peeping from underneath her wedding gown just made her lovelier.

No!

'It's your wedding night, Tom,' she said softly, and crossed to take the glasses from his hands. 'Leave them.'

'I—' He took a huge intake of air, fighting for strength. She was so lovely. 'You should be in bed,' he told her, and if his voice didn't sound right who could blame him? He was holding himself so rigid he thought he'd snap.

'I know I should.' And then she put her hands on his shoulders and her eyes met his—almost defiant. 'I've asked you before and now I'm asking you again. Take me.'

'I—' He shook himself and backed away but she didn't release him. She followed, her hands still on his shoulders—as if they were still dancing. As if they were still one.

'Tom, what are you frightened of?'

'I'm not frightened.'

'You're brave enough,' she said, as if she hadn't heard him. 'You fight your oil-well fires. Surely the danger you face there can't be worse than falling in love?'

'In love?'

'I love you, Tom Bradley,' she said simply. 'It's the cold, hard truth. I never thought I'd say it. After Chris...well, I thought I felt love for Chris. I was wrong. I was stupid and naive and far, far too young to know what love was. What I feel for you is a million light-years away from that, and you're standing there, treating me as if I'm a blazing fire myself. More frightening than any oil well.'

'I told you, Rose,' he said harshly and his hands came up and caught hers, putting her away from him. 'I'm not in the market for commitment.'

'Yet you want it.' She was as watchful as a cat, noting his every expression. 'You want me.'

'No!'

'Why not, Tom?'

'Hell, it doesn't matter.' He broke away and turned so that he wasn't facing her, looking instead out of the darkened window to the valley beyond. 'I'm not committing here, Rose. I can't. You'll go.'

Silence. And then…'Where will I go?' Rose asked softly. 'Just where will I go, Tom Bradley?'

'Anywhere. I don't know. It happens.'

'No.'

'Don't you understand?' he demanded, and his anger surged. He twisted himself round to face her. 'Don't you see? I've killed it. Any chance I had of being able to form a long-term relationship died a long time ago. All my life— there were such great people. My mother had such a good line in lovers, in families. They were people who wanted me, loved me. And every time it ended.'

'Your mother did that,' she said calmly. 'That was your mother's doing. This time it's you who's being asked to make the decision.'

He stared down at her. 'No. I've tried. Even Marty…'

'Marty died,' she said softly. 'And I can't help that. I can't make any guarantees about calamities. But here, this is your family and we love you. Even if I died, there's still Jess and Toby and Yoghurt—and seven puppies—and all the love in the world. We're all just waiting for you to love us back.'

'Rose.'

She crossed the room, silent as a ghost on her bare toes, and she put her hands up to cup his face with her fingers. She stood on tiptoe and her lips were so close to his that he could feel her breath.

'You're loved, Tom Bradley,' she said softly. 'Despite yourself, you're one of us. You've fought and fought, but you've lost the fight so you might as well surrender. You've married me. I'm not Rose Allen any more. I'm Rose Bradley—your wife. I'm half of your whole. Sensible or not, I've married you—for better or for worse—and I don't

take my vows lightly. Nor am I prepared to be a wife in
name only. I want it all.'

'Rose, I can't.' His words were almost a groan, but she
simply smiled. Her hands tightened on his face and she
tilted her face further, so her lips were brushing his.

'You mean…you're standing here and saying you don't
want me?'

'No. Yes, but… Rose, hell…'

'Don't swear at your wife,' she said serenely. 'At least,
not in front of the children. Take me to bed.'

'I don't—'

'You're saying I only have a tiny single bed,' she said—
and for heaven's sake she was laughing at him! 'So I did.
But come and see my wedding gift to you.'

And before he knew what she was about, before he could
come up with any of the hundreds of counter-arguments
crowding in his brain, she took his hand and led him out
of the room. Her hand was firm and insistent, leading him
forth.

'Where…?'

'Hush and see.'

And she led him to the front of the house, to a room that
until yesterday had been bare of any furniture at all. She
swung the door wide and flicked on the lamp—and Tom
stared.

It was no longer empty. It was filled almost to bursting
with a vast four-poster bed, made up with old-fashioned
quilts, mounds and mounds of pillows and creamy white
linen. It looked wonderful. Old and comfortable and incredibly inviting. It looked—

It looked as if it was just waiting.

'What—? Where—where on earth did this come from?'
His voice was almost a croak.

'It came this morning,' she said gently, 'while you were
feeding the cows. The bed belonged to my parents. I'd

placed it for sale in the local antique shop but no one had bought it yet. I guess most people think it's too big. Not me. Not for the purpose I think it should be used for. This morning I asked Bob Mitchell to bring it home.'

'Rose.' The air was threatening to choke him. He was stifled. Fighting something he didn't understand.

And he was losing.

'This wasn't Chris's and my bed,' she said softly, her fingers stroking his. 'He wanted a modern bed, a water-bed, for heaven's sake. But somehow—somehow I knew you'd love this.'

'I don't. I can't.'

'You do. You can!'

'Rose Allen, are you trying to seduce me?' he said in a strangled voice, and she chuckled.

'No way. Rose Allen couldn't possibly seduce Tom Bradley. But Rose Bradley, wife of Tom Bradley—now that's another story.'

'Rose…'

'Do you really not want me?' she asked in a throaty whisper, and her arms came up and entwined themselves around his neck. She stood on tiptoes and kissed him—lightly on the lips at first, and then more deeply. 'Really?'

'I can't.'

'You can,' she said simply. Her hand fell to the open buttons at her breast, and she undid the remaining fastenings one by one, watching his face as she did so. The sensation she evoked was unbearably sexy.

Unbearably…

He should leave.

He couldn't move to save himself.

Her bodice fell to her waist. She unclipped her bra and that, too, fell away. It dropped to the floor and lay unnoticed.

Her eyes didn't leave his.

'I want you, Tom Bradley,' she said, and her voice was a husky whisper, breathless with desire. 'I've wanted you from the moment I set eyes on you. I love you and you're my husband. I'm your wife, and I want you to take me to our wedding bed. Where I belong.'

'Rose, I'm not staying,' he managed, trying to drag his eyes from her. 'You know I can't.'

'I know that,' she said calmly. 'You work overseas and when you work you can't be here. I accept that. Tomorrow you can do anything you want. But for tonight…for tonight you're mine.'

And her fingers finished with the last of the buttons. Her dress fell into a soft mound of silken folds on the polished floorboards, and she was standing before him. His bride.

There was a wisp of silken lace that was her panties. Nothing more… And while he watched she slipped her fingers into them and let the last of the lace fall away.

'Take me, Tom,' she whispered. 'Please…'

Dear God. It was the *please* that got to him. Anything else… if she'd said anything else…

But to walk away now…

He closed his eyes, and she took two steps forward and took him in her arms—and held him to her heart.

'Now?'

'Rose, are you sure?' he groaned. His self-control was stretched so thin, he was within a hair's breadth of snapping. 'You know I'll walk away. I can't stay here for ever. I'll leave. I must, and I don't want to hurt you.'

'You won't walk away tonight, Tom,' she whispered. 'For tonight, you're my husband. My man. I've been alone for so long, and I need you like life itself. So take me. Love me. My Tom.'

And he looked down at her in the dim light and could stand it no longer. There were some things no man could resist—and she was so, so lovely.

She was his wife.

His love.

With a groan he gathered her to him, and lifted her glorious body into his arms, against his chest—against his heart.

The big bed was waiting—waiting to claim its own. It was a marriage bed, and in this house today there'd been a marriage. A man and a woman becoming one.

Tom Bradley could resist no longer.

They fell together, their lips pressed, her body curling into his, suppliant and yet demanding—aching for her man.

Her man.

Tom.

CHAPTER EIGHT

ROSE woke before dawn. In the other room one of the twins was stirring. Lovely, she thought dreamily. Six whole hours' sleep.

Give or take an hour. Or more. An hour or more of love.

Her body was cradled against Tom's, and his arms held her loosely in sleep. She was curved into him as if she belonged there, the line of her back curled into his breast— skin against skin.

He smelled good. He felt good.

No. He felt great!

She'd never felt like this, she thought dreamily. She felt loved, desired and fulfilled. Tom was everything and more she'd ever dreamed a lover could be. Tender and yet strong, patient and yet urgent—as intent on her pleasure as he was on his own.

And pleasure she'd had. She'd thought she'd be tender after the twins—that there might be pain—but there'd been nothing but sheer, exquisite joy in their coupling.

It was right. He was her man.

Toby whimpered again, but she didn't want to move. She snuggled against her husband, and his arms tightened in drowsiness, his lips brushing her hair almost subconsciously.

'Nice,' he growled. 'Stay…' And he disappeared again into sleep.

Stay… He was asking *her* to stay. There was a turna-round!

And even that was impossible, she thought ruefully. There was work to be done. Twins to be fed.

Loving could wait—for a little. A very little!

She twisted within his hold to kiss him lovingly on the nose—a wifely gesture of proprietorship—and then wriggled free, ignoring his groan of protest and padding through the empty house to the kitchen. She collected the twins as she went. Tom had moved their cribs into the next-door bedroom some time the night before, after they'd realised he wouldn't be returning to his sofa-bed in the kitchen.

'Because if I'm not around to referee we'll have pups in the baby baskets and babies in the dog basket,' he'd said, pulling himself away from Rose for about thirty seconds while he organised it.

That was so like Tom, Rose thought contentedly. He was so thoughtful! How many men would make love and then manage to consider the babies' welfare before drifting off to sleep? Or—as had happened—before making love again!

Her Tom. Her lovely, lovely Tom!

'He must stay,' she told Toby as she lifted her tiny son from his crib. 'We must see how we can make him stay. He's your daddy—more than Chris could ever have been. He loves you. He loves us.'

He didn't think he could love.

'And that's nonsense,' she said fiercely, so fiercely that Yoghurt raised her sleepy head by the fire and looked across in concern. 'He *can* love. He's just afraid...afraid we'll hurt him. Afraid he'll hurt us.'

Surely he couldn't think that any more?

Tom woke as she left. For a while he didn't move, just lay savouring the warmth of the bedclothes, the feeling of his skin where she'd lain against him, the smell of her.

Rose...

He'd made love to women before, but never like this. Never had he felt like this! She was the most perfect, the most wonderful woman.

Could he stay?

Maybe.

He rolled over and stretched, then lay listening to the sounds of morning. There was a cow near the house, welcoming the dawn with her gentle lowing. A rooster was doing the same, but the noise it was making wasn't as gentle. He heard Rose moving as she tended to the twins, the soft murmur of her voice indistinct but soothing as she chatted to her babies and her dogs.

It was all…perfect.

But he'd felt like this before. Maybe not as much as this, he thought bleakly, but nearly. Once before, there'd been a farm. It had belonged to his third—or was it his fourth?—stepdad. The man had been wonderful. He'd taught Tom to fish and had taken him around the farm, showing him all he knew. Tom had been six or maybe seven, and he'd been in small-boy heaven. For once, he'd figured, his mother had got it right.

Then Christmas had come, and he'd woken and found a pony in the side paddock. Her name was Blacky and she was all his. Henry, her mother's new partner, had said so. 'She's your own horse, boy. Your first. My gift to you. Treat her right and we'll see what sort of horseman we can make of you.'

Tom had gone to sleep that night so happy he'd felt almost ill—and the next morning he'd woken to find his mother stony-faced and packing.

'Let's face it, I'm not a housewife,' she'd snapped when Tom had dared to question her. 'I'm not destined to belong to any man. This place is getting to me, and if he thinks he's buying me by being nice to you…'

Henry never had a chance. They'd been out of there before Tom knew what hit him, and he hadn't even had time to say goodbye to Blacky.

This place is getting to me...

Maybe I'm like that, Tom thought bleakly. How the hell can I stay here? I know how claustrophobic this makes me feel.

It didn't. This morning it didn't. It just made him feel—good!

Well, it will, he said to himself savagely as he headed for the shower. Any minute now it'll close in on me, so if I let myself get any closer...

It was too late. He already had.

And then...

'So she learns to depend on me.' He was talking out loud now under the falling water, and he didn't like what he was hearing one bit. 'She's open for loving. She's vulnerable and I know it. I'll let her depend on me and then I'll get that damned feeling my mother had...

'I might not,' he answered himself.

'I will!'

So go now!

The knowledge hit him like a sledgehammer. He'd done what he'd set out to do. He'd married Rose, and he'd made her safe. Now he could keep her financially secure, and from time to time, when the world got too bleak, he'd come home for a lightning visit.

And they'd be here.

It's hardly fair on them, he told himself harshly. To expect them to be here waiting.

They need you financially. Without you they'd be in a mess. There's no way they'd stay on the farm. So, you can support them in any way they need—just not emotionally.

But there were flaws in his logic. Last night was one.

What had happened between him and Rose didn't fit into any sort of sensible agreement.

So last night should never have happened, and you know it, he said to himself. And it'll happen again if you stay. You've done some stupid things in your life, Tom Bradley, but you've never been knowingly cruel. If you let Rose love you...

She already does.

The little voice whispered in his ear, insidious in its sweetness. *She already does...*

Well, quit making it worse! He twisted off the hot tap, making the water pouring onto his chest icy cold. It was so cold it hurt, and he welcomed the pain. You know damned well it's only going to get worse, he told himself savagely. You have to get out until you calm down. Until you can look at her without wanting her, and...and it all just settles.

It won't settle. That voice again.

It must. So get yourself out of here and give logic a chance.

Go!

She didn't understand.

Rose stood stony-faced while Tom tried to explain things to her. Hell, he even told her about Blacky.

'So there's no fire you're rushing off to,' she said carefully, wiping her wet hands on the dishcloth and facing him with eyes that were blank with hurt. 'There's no reason.'

'I told you.'

'You told me you'd marry me and you'd leave us,' she said. 'But you'd leave us at need. Go off and save the world when it needed saving, and come back to us between times. But there's no world out there that needs saving now.'

'I'll contact my boss. Charlie—'

'He'll find you a world to save?'

'No, but…'

'So you'll tell him that you'll be staying in some motel room, poised at the ready, fire extinguisher loaded.'

He tried to smile but it didn't work. 'Something like that,' he admitted. 'I can't stay here. Not…feeling like I do.'

'Which is?'

He took a deep breath. 'Feeling as if I'm falling in love with you.'

There. He'd said it, but it wasn't right. His heart numbed at the words. They were dead wrong.

Love? For him? No and no and no!

But she didn't see. 'Is that such a crime?' she asked, her eyes resting on his. She was wearing a flimsy lacy night-dress she'd put on for her wedding night—or rather for her wedding morning, because last night she'd needed no such adornment. Her eyes were huge in her too pale face, and her breast was rising and falling—she was breathing too fast.

It was as if she was struggling against odds that were loaded against her.

'I'll hurt you, Rose.'

'If you walk away now,' she said slowly, 'then you'll hurt me.'

'I never made any promises.'

'You did last night. You loved me.'

'I was stupid,' he said angrily. 'I never meant this. I only want a marriage in name.'

'Do you think your mother was afraid, too?' she said softly, taking a new tack. 'Do you think that's why you were torn away?'

'I don't know.'

'I don't think you're worrying about me being hurt,' she told him. 'I think it's plain cowardice on your part. You're too scared to admit you need me.'

'Rose.'

'We need each other, Tom,' she said softly. 'We've known each other for over five weeks now, but I didn't have to know you for five minutes before I could tell. I love you and I want you—and you're my husband. That's the way I feel. If you go and skulk in some motel room...'

'Hey, I'm not skulking.'

'Skulking,' she said, and for the first time there was anger blazing behind her eyes. 'Hiding from the truth. Well, you go and be miserable wherever you want, but it won't make you one whit less married. It won't make you one whit less my husband. Wherever you go, wherever you are, know that we love you and your place is here. With your family. Your home.'

'Rose.'

She turned her back on him and when she spoke again there were tears in her voice. She was damned if she'd let him see them, though. Her shoulders were set and when he reached out to touch her she wrenched away in anger.

'Go on, get out of here,' she said bitterly. 'Off you go and start your isolation.'

'I don't...'

'Tom!' She whirled to face him, and her expression was pleading. 'Tom, I can't handle this,' she said, her voice breaking. 'Please, if you're going, just go. Go and be cowardly somewhere else.'

'I'm not—'

'A coward?' She gave a furious gasp, clenching her hands by her sides until her fingers whitened. 'Oh, yes, you are. You can cope with hell-fire and drama and childbirth, and even the odd nappy change... but you can't cope with the most important thing of all. You can't cope with love!'

'There's nothing on.'

'What do you mean, there's nothing on?' Tom demanded. 'Something has to be.'

'Nope. There's a bit of a burn on down in Mexico but—'

'So send me there.'

'Steve's already in charge.'

'Huh!'

'Steve's more than capable,' Charlie said easily. 'Just because he's five years younger than you that doesn't mean he's less fit for the job. He's got a good head on his shoulders, and reflexes that should make you proud of your training.'

'Yeah, but…'

'I know he trained under you,' Charlie said firmly. 'But maybe that's what this job's all about: Getting your experience and then moving into training and organisational mode before your luck runs out.'

'I need a fire, Charlie.'

'So what do you want me to do about it?' Charlie sighed. 'You want me to bomb an oil well? Organise a little war in the Gulf, just to satisfy your pyromania?'

'No, but—'

'Come back to Houston and we'll see about getting you a desk job.'

'A desk job! In your dreams!'

Charlie laughed, but there was a note of concern behind the laughter. 'So what've you been doing with your vacation, then? A few beers and a few women, I hope.'

'Just the one.' It was out before he knew he intended saying it, and the sudden quiet at the end of the line told him he'd made a mistake.

'Just the one?' Charlie's voice was intent—like Yoghurt hitting a scent. Charlie wasn't in charge of the biggest oil-fire outfit in the world for nothing. His intelligence was awesome and now he put it to use. 'It's not *just the one* beer,' he said slowly. 'Some things stretch credibility too far. So if it's not *just the one* beer then it's *just the one* woman. You want to tell Uncle Charlie all?'

'No.'

'Whoa…' Charlie whistled down the phone, and Tom could practically see his ears prick and his keen eyes narrow. Where his team was concerned, he wanted to know everything. 'Name?'

'Rose, but…'

'My Maddie's middle name is Rose,' Charlie said with pleasure. 'You thinking of marrying?'

'Yeah,' Tom said tightly. 'I already did.'

'You already did?' Charlie's voice went blank. 'Well, I'll be pickled…'

'Yeah, and I've had twins…'

'In five weeks and a bit!'

'I move fast,' Tom told him. 'First I had septuplets, and then the twins. But now I've been there, done that, and I want out.'

'You're kidding me.' Charlie's voice dropped off in disappointment. 'Hell, you had me going there.'

'So give me a job.'

'There isn't really a Rose?'

'Give me a job, Charlie.'

Charlie sighed. 'You got the mobile phone turned on?'

'I got the mobile.'

'I'll see what I can do. If you want to blow yourself up—well, there are times I wouldn't mind letting you try. Stupid young fool. If there's not really a Rose, you sure as hell need to find one.'

He needed no such thing, Tom thought darkly as he replaced the receiver. He'd gotten out before he'd buried himself in emotion so deep he would never have been able to dig himself out. He'd gotten out while the going was good.

So now... Now he could lie on the beach a bit longer, drink a few beers, eye some women in the bar...

Ha! There wasn't a woman in the country he wanted to look at! Except for Rose.

So all he could do was wait for Charlie's call to come, and it had better come soon—because he was going nuts!

He was nuts because all he wanted to do was head back to Rose.

In the end, though, it was Rose who contacted him before Charlie.

He'd left her his mobile phone number—'just in case of emergencies... one of the twins or something...' His voice had trailed off as he'd said it, knowing how futile it sounded, and he had never imagined she'd use it.

Now he came back from a morning swim—he was staying in some beachfront hotel and swimming was the only way he knew how to lose some of his restless energy—to find his phone message bank flashing red.

Charlie! Thank God! He practically lunged across the room to hit the replay button, and then felt his chest knot at the sound of Rose's recorded voice.

'Tom, there's a real problem here. Ring me.'

It took him two seconds to dial her number, visions of dead twins flashing before his eyes. Or bailiffs. Or someone breaking and entering the farmhouse. Rape and pillage. Or a fire.

Hell, by the time she answered he'd gone through every catastrophe known to man.

'Rose?' His voice came out sounding ridiculously strained, and she heard his anxiety.

'Hey, Tom, calm down.'

'The twins...'

'The twins are fine.'

'You...'

'I'm fine, too. Where are you?'

'Sydney. Manly Beach.'

'Oh.' She hesitated a bit, and when she next spoke he heard relief. 'I thought—I thought you might be overseas already.'

He should be. Maybe the sensible thing would have been to have headed back to the US and Charlie's desk job. Instead he was still within driving distance of Rose.

Stupid!

'I'm not,' he said shortly. 'Tell me what's wrong.'

'It's silly to bother you—' she faltered '—it's just... It's Yoghurt.'

'Yoghurt!'

'She hasn't eaten since you left,' Rose told him. 'She just sits and pines. I've weaned the pups so she's not feeding them—otherwise she'd be dead by now—but she just sits and looks at the door.'

Hell. Yoghurt starving? But...she was only a dog.

'There's not a lot I can do about that,' Tom said slowly.

Rose sighed. 'No. I suppose not.'

'You've taken her to the vet?'

'Of course I have!'

'What did he say?'

'He said she's one depressed bloodhound. He says she's probably pining for a previous life—someone she loved must have owned her once. She cheered up a bit when she got attached to you, but then you went... You deserted her, too.'

He didn't believe this! All the angst he was feeling, and he had to worry about the angst of a dog! But, curiously, he did.

'You're feeding her steak?' he demanded. 'There's plenty of money. You're not giving her that dried muck?'

'I'm giving her steak,' she said indignantly. 'I don't feel guilty about using your money to feed your dog.'

'She's not my dog.'

'So whose dog is she?'

'Yours,' he said generously, and she sighed.

'Nice try, Tom—' her voice was sad again '—but it's not as easy as that. You can't just switch off emotion. Leave money for a few steaks and leave.'

'I'm not—'

'Yoghurt's pining for you,' she said bluntly. 'And the vet thinks she'll die if she doesn't cheer up.'

'You're kidding!'

'Would I kid about something as important as this?' Rose's voice grew angry. 'She's here now, her head is draped over my bare feet while I'm talking to you, and she's looking at me. Just looking at me. With those great wet eyes. You want me to send you a video so you can see?'

'No.'

'She's your dog, Tom. You rescued her and you brought her here. Come back and look after her.'

'I can't do that.' Bleak, hard, unanswerable.

'Then tell me it's okay to have her put down,' Rose snapped. 'You tell me that, Tom Bradley, because I'm damned if I'm sitting here watching her starve herself to death because of your selfishness!'

Selfishness...

Tom spent a long time staring at the hotel ceiling and trying to figure out whether she was right or not. Was it selfishness that had made him walk away?

No! It wasn't selfishness. He'd been more than generous in marrying her!

But that was his head talking, he acknowledged, not his heart—and he knew his head was a liar. Generosity had had nothing to do with it. The truth was that he'd married her because he couldn't bear not to. He couldn't bear the thought that she would be alone and vulnerable and open to the hurts of the world.

She was lovely and she was desirable—she'd agreed to marry him and she'd wanted him to stay.

So was he selfish? No, he decided, it was more than that. Sure, he was afraid he'd be hurt if he got any more deeply entangled emotionally. But it went deeper than that. Like mother, like son, he thought bleakly, and if he let Rose depend on him, if he let the twins think of him as their dad—and then he couldn't take the claustrophobia of domestic ties and walked away...

Maybe he wouldn't feel claustrophobic.

Yeah, right, he told himself savagely. You were feeling it after five weeks! Total commitment. Really good, Bradley!

You didn't feel claustrophobic after you made love to her, that other inner voice of his whispered back.

But it'll come. It'll return. It always does.

He got up and took a few quick paces around the room—and then another ten or so. Okay. He made himself calm down. He wasn't being logical here, and he needed to be. There was still a real danger that the claustrophobia would come and he wasn't risking that. He wouldn't risk hurting her by going back—at least not permanently—but there was an added problem now.

One anorexic bloodhound called Yoghurt.

She's just a stray, he tried to tell himself, but he didn't even get the word 'stray' to form in his mind. His brain stalled mid-word and froze. Yoghurt wasn't a stray. She was Yoghurt. One droopy dog, hauling herself up onto his couch and licking him while he slept. One sad-eyed blood-

hound asking to be taken up on his truck tray, looking at
him with eyes that were aching to adore.

Oh, for heaven's sake, she's only a dog! he told himself
crossly. If she's so damned stupid...

Then you have to do something about it.

Why?

She loves you.

No. She loves something in the past. I'm just a replace-
ment—second-best for what she's already lost.

That was a bright note. The vet had said she'd loved
someone before. That had him sitting down on his too big
hotel bed and starting to plan. There couldn't be all that
many bloodhounds in this country called Yoghurt, but he
and Rose had placed an advertisement in the newspaper the
week after the pups were born and no one had come forward.

'She's probably been abandoned,' Rose had said, and
since both of them had sort of wanted to keep her—or
rather *really* wanted to keep her—then they'd done nothing
else about it.

But if Tom were to pull out all the stops...

Why would someone abandon a dog like Yoghurt? he
asked himself—and he had to grin. All sorts of reasons
sprang to mind. But whoever it was must have loved her
in the first place, or been attached to someone who loved
her. If he could find them...

How?

Try money, he told himself. After all, that's what you're
good at. That's what you're doing with Rose, isn't it?
Paying to keep yourself out of trouble?

His grin faded.

You're getting too cynical for your own good, he told
himself bleakly. This is crazy. Just get your money working
and solve Yoghurt's problem.

It might mean visiting the farm again.

It won't kill you.

It sure wouldn't. His gut kicked at the thought of a visit. He'd been gone now for a week. A week was a long time in the life of the twins. They might even be smiling.

Would they smile like their mother?

Cut it out, he told himself firmly, and started throwing things into his hold-all. Just keep the emotion out of it. You're going h— I mean you're going back to the farm to solve the problem of one bloodhound—and that's all!

'He'll come.'

Rose replaced the receiver and knelt down to take the big dog's face in her hands. If he doesn't... But he will...

'If he doesn't,' she said resolutely, 'then we'll just have to cope, Yoghurt, girl. We can get along without men. We have before.'

Yoghurt looked up at her, the lost dreams of the universe drowning in her eyes, and it was all Rose could do not to break down and howl.

'You'd fail as a feminist,' she said crossly, taking herself firmly in hand. 'Pining because of some man. We women have come a long way...'

We bloodhounds obviously hadn't. Rose sighed and went across to chop a little steak. She brought it back, and Yoghurt sighed, too.

She didn't eat.

'Pining for love is just ridiculous,' Rose told her. 'There's nothing special about Tom Bradley.'

Who do you think you're kidding?

CHAPTER NINE

IT TOOK Tom three days before he made it to the farm and those three days were spent in the most intensive sleuthing he'd ever done. He paid money for a blitz of advertising, he followed false leads, he interviewed a few extremely odd people.

And finally he met a dog. A dog who looked almost as depressed as Yoghurt.

'She'll kill me,' he told the dog as he ushered the flea-bitten bag of bones into his newly hired little car and pointed the car farmwards.

But he knew he was right. Well, maybe he *hoped* he was right.

It took courage to go home. On arrival he paused before the turn into the farm, and sat for a long time out on the road, staring down the driveway. His money was already at work. Before he'd left, he'd started putting the farm into order and there had been more done since he'd been gone. The whole place had been completely painted, profession-als finishing what he'd started. It looked bright, cheerful and homely, tucked away behind its canopy of trees.

It looked prosperous. It also looked incredibly welcom-ing.

'I'm only here to visit,' he told the dog at his side. 'Not like you. With luck, you're here to stay, at least until we can find someone who'll keep you long-term. If you play your cards right…'

The dog looked up at him as if luck was something that didn't enter his vocabulary.

'So try to smile,' Tom suggested. 'She likes a smile.'

She has a really beautiful smile all of her own…

Bradley, keep your mind on the job at hand, he said to himself sternly. Nothing else. Deliver a dog and then get the heck out of here.

You're her husband.

'In name only,' he said aloud. 'You have visiting rights. That's all.'

The dog looked up at him as if he were crazy, and that was exactly how he felt. Crazy!

Rose took a while answering after he knocked. Tom could hear a twin snuffling inside, and he felt an almost irresistible urge to walk right in, but, 'I'm only here as a visitor,' he told the dog at his side, and focussed on fixing his smile into a nice formal greeting. *Husband coming home from the war, but preparing to be off again by lunchtime.*

By the time she came his face was aching from smiling, but when she finally swung the door wide his effort was all for nothing.

His smile died. It was inane to smile when his gut was kicking so hard.

Seeing her *hurt*, and he couldn't believe how much!

She was wearing her customary old jeans and a baggy, oversized man's shirt. Her feet were bare, and her hair was freshly washed and *so* pretty—the way it curled like that, twisting into tiny tendrils at the nape of her neck. As she looked at him with an oddly twisting smile of surprise and pleasure and wariness, all he wanted to do was to sweep her into his arms and hug her.

Instead—somehow—he stayed where he was and contented himself with just looking.

Her smile died as well. Her eyes slowly dulled with shock—and pain.

'Tom.'

It was only a word. It just felt like a caress, and it had no business feeling like that.

Silence.

It went on and on, with each of them frozen like statues.

The dog moved first, restlessly shifting against Tom's leg. Rose looked down and her eyes widened at what she saw.

'Another bloodhound,' she said blankly.

'I brought him for you.'

She stared up at him again at that, and her look changed to match his stupid attempt at a greeting—*wife greeting husband home from war who'd clearly left his senses back on the battlefield.*

'You brought me a dog.'

'His name's Boris,' Tom said helpfully, and her expression didn't change one bit.

'Do you make a habit,' she said carefully, 'of going around the country collecting stray bloodhounds? And dumping them on my doorstep?'

'You want me to explain?'

'Maybe you should.'

'I could come in,' he suggested, and she nodded and stepped aside to let him past.

'Of course. You know this place is yours.'

'I'm only leasing it from the twins.' That had been the legal arrangement. It made Rose absolutely secure where she was, no one could take her home from her and the money could go into a trust account for the twins' education.

'Yeah. You're leasing it.' Her voice was expressionless as she followed him. 'So come in…to your leased home. Would you like to do a landlord's inspection?'

'Rose.'

'Go on in!' There was anger behind the curt words and

Tom flinched as he opened the door to the kitchen. Boris Bloodhound dragged himself in beside him, and Yoghurt looked up apathetically from her bed beside the fire.

And then something extraordinary happened.

First Yoghurt saw Tom. He'd spoken, she recognised the sound of his voice, and her tail started a slow, half-hearted wag as she rose to her feet.

And then her eyes dropped to the creature at his side—and she saw Boris.

For one long moment she stood motionless, her whole body quivering, every sense taking in what was before her. She stared and stared. Then Boris Bloodhound took a tentative step towards her—

And Yoghurt was out of her basket as if it were on fire, her whole body launching forward, her ears streaming back, her tail flattening like a pointer. She gave a high-pitched yelp, skittered across the room and stopped short three inches from Boris's nose.

Once more there was silence.

Both dogs stood motionless, checking each other out. Then Yoghurt leaned forward those three short inches, her scraggy body sagging with the effort. She sniffed and sniffed again—and so did Boris.

And suddenly the apathy was completely gone. So was the vision of two sad, bedraggled, world-weary bloodhounds. Yoghurt gave a joyful, ear-splitting bark. Then she yelped and yelped again, and Boris joined right in—and then the dogs launched themselves at each other, leaping and tumbling, licking, sniffing, falling, clambering, for all the world like two carefree puppies rather than two careworn dogs.

Tom and Rose were left to watch—and wonder. Their own tumultuous emotions were momentarily set aside in the face of this transformation.

'Yoghurt's tail,' Rose said in awe, staring down at the

mass of dog flesh tumbling around her legs. 'Look at her tail!'

Look? How could Tom miss it? Yoghurt's tail was whirling like a helicopter blade, wagging so hard it was a wonder she didn't take off. Her ears were flying, her big head was lolling back and forth, there was spittle flying everywhere...

'Ugh!' Rose said faintly. 'My new paintwork. I don't think...'

'Well, I do,' Tom said, grinning. 'And I'm thinking what you're thinking. No matter how touching this scene is, I think that the rest of their reunion might be done outside.' He grabbed their two collars and hauled his charges out onto the porch, where they took right up from where they had left off, tumbling, yelping, and then racing in crazy circles round and round the outside of the house, delirious in their delight.

'You know,' Rose said carefully, watching them spin past for the third time, 'I get a weird suspicion that these two dogs might just have met each other before.'

Tom grinned again. 'Whatever makes you think that?'

Rose choked on a bubble of laughter, and then somehow schooled her face back into solemnity. She put her hands on her hips and managed a glare. 'Are you intending to tell me?'

Tell her? Of course, but first he had to get his voice in order. Switch his thoughts right back to dogs. Tom looked at her and she was just as gorgeous as ever, standing there with her hands on her hips, and with her lips trying to hold back a chuckle. She was trying so hard to be mad at him and it wasn't working.

Thank heavens for that. He didn't like it when she was angry.

He'd never wanted to hurt her, and he was doing it now, he thought suddenly—by not loving her.

'Yoghurt's real name's not Yoghurt,' he said hurriedly, transferring his attention hastily back to the two dogs. He had to look at something other than Rose!

'Not Yoghurt?'

'It's T-Bone.'

'Yeah?'

'Yes.'

'You're not,' she said slowly, 'making this up?'

'Why would I do that?'

'I don't know. Maybe to talk me into keeping another dog?'

'I never meant to bring another dog. I wouldn't do that to you.'

'I think you just have,' she said carefully. 'So we have a dog called Boris and another dog called T-Bone alias Yoghurt. Are you planning to elaborate?'

'Yeah.' It was so hard to keep focussed on dogs, but he must! 'I...'

'I?'

For heaven's sake, he was sounding like a gibbering schoolboy. He made a massive effort and somehow managed to clear the fuzz in his head—the fuzz that was distracting him just because she'd chuckled in a way that made his heart twist.

'Both the dogs belonged to a very old lady who lived in Kingston,' he told her. 'She named them Boris and T-Bone. Two bloodhounds with impeccable pedigrees. She doted on them, and spent all her pension on feeding them. The more frail she grew, though, the more impossible it was for her to look after them. She paid a local girl to walk them every afternoon, and then, when she had a heart attack, she asked Melissa if she'd take them home and care for them permanently.'

'Melissa?'

'Melissa is unemployed, and unendowed in the brains

department,' Tom said carefully. 'She was living in a communal house of peace-loving, pot-smoking vegans. She earns her only income from odd jobs like caring for Boris and T-Bone, and what she lacks in the brains department she makes up for with her heart. Even though she.couldn't afford it, she could no sooner knock back the request to care for the dogs than she could fly, so she took them in—and then the old lady died.'

'I see,' Rose said slowly, staring out at the settling dogs. They'd stilled, and Yoghurt was starting to sniff every single inch of Boris's scraggy form.

Was it Tom's imagination or was she avoiding looking at him? Maybe... Or maybe it was just that he wanted her to be as churned up as he was. For some stupid, totally inexplicable reason...

'So then what?' she asked, and he had to haul his thoughts back together.

'They changed T-Bone's name to Yoghurt—of course,' Tom told her. 'T-Bone wouldn't fit into a house of vegans, and they had principles. They started feeding both dogs a diet of pasta. Nothing else, I gather. Just pasta. Then they figured that the bloodhounds had good pedigrees so they'd breed from them, but of course there was no money for vet advice. But Yoghurt—T-Bone—got pregnant anyway.'

'And then?'

'Then Melissa got a new boyfriend and moved out of the house. The boyfriend didn't like dogs so she left Boris and T-Bone behind. The others in the house didn't seem to notice the dogs and they began to starve. Finally I guess Yoghurt—T-Bone—got so desperate she took off, trying to find someplace to have her pups where she had a chance of a feed.'

'And that's where we came in?'

'That's where we came in,' Tom said grimly. 'The first time we advertised for her owner I don't think anyone in the house was capable of reading the paper. Then, after the first few glorious weeks of cohabiting with her new lover, Melissa had a conscience pang and went back to check on the dogs—and only found Boris. The new boyfriend seems quite a decent bloke. Even though he doesn't like dogs, he didn't want to see them starve so he agreed that they'd take Boris home, and they started searching for T-Bone. It was he who saw my advertisement this week and rang me.'

'So...' Rose's eyes widened as she took this in, but she still didn't look at him. 'So Melissa still cares. Does she want her back?' she asked in a small voice.

'Does she want Yoghurt—I mean T-Bone?'

'Mmm.'

'I would have thought that you'd be pleased to be shot of her,' Tom said. 'I mean, she's a real responsibility.'

'It's not me who runs from responsibilities,' Rose snapped. 'Does she want her?' There was raw anxiety in her voice.

'No.'

'Thank heaven for that.' Her breath came out in a rush. 'And— and Boris? I can keep Boris?'

'You mean you want to keep him as well?'

'Of course I do,' she said solidly. 'You couldn't separate these two. They love each other.'

'I thought maybe I could advertise for a good home. They'd be happy if we kept them together and they do have impeccable pedigrees.'

'You mean you'd sell them?' Rose demanded incredulously. 'For money?'

'I don't mean anything of the kind.' Tom sighed and looked at her—mistake!—and looked away again. 'I mean, I don't want to saddle you with any more encumbrances.'

'You haven't saddled me with enough.'

'What's that supposed to mean?' But he knew. Without doubt he knew, and it had been a stupid question. It hung around them in the warm afternoon air, while the dogs slowly settled into blissful rest at their feet. Inside the house Tom could hear the sound of a dozen or so desperate little paws against the screen doors—T-Bone's puppies aching to join their mother—and there was a twin gurgling away in a distant cot.

It felt like home!

It was no such thing. He gave himself a fierce mental shake and it didn't do an ounce of good at all.

The gurgle turned into a wail.

'Toby's waiting to be fed,' Rose said, looking down at her bare toes. 'You'd best come back in. I'll put the kettle on. You can make us a cup of tea while I feed. That is—' she flashed him an uncertain glance '—if you have time. If it won't make you late for your dinner back at your hotel. Or some other imperative need.'

'Rose.'

She ignored him and stalked up the porch steps, her dignity only ruffled when she opened the screen door. Seven fat puppies came flying out, wrapping themselves around her legs in delight and their eagerness to join in. She stepped over them, they tumbled on down towards their mother, and she would have gone indoors and left them to it—but one puppy didn't quite make it.

He'd leapt up on Rose's leg, staggered backwards, hit one of his brothers and sisters—and then slithered sideways through the gap in the steps and underneath the house.

His yelp as he disappeared into darkness was truly heart-rending.

Rose swore.

'These puppies,' she said conversationally, 'are going to be the death of me. We should have named them Trouble One to Trouble Seven. Now what?' She knelt on the bottom step and peered into the darkness.

Somewhere from the dark, a puppy wuffled back.

'It can't get out,' she said ominously. 'The gaps between the lower steps are too narrow. It fell through the top one and it can't climb up to reach it.'

T-Bone wandered over to see. She nuzzled Rose, then stuck her nose between the steps and whined in motherly concern. Do something about it, her whine said.

'Never mind, Yoghurt—I mean T-Bone,' Rose said, brightening. She straightened and brushed the dust off her jeans. 'You know I told you we don't need men? It seems I was wrong. You need a man to cheer you up, I need a man to retrieve your puppy. Tom Bradley!'

Tom started. 'Yes, ma'am.'

'Retrieve this puppy,' she ordered. 'I have twins to feed and steak to carve for two hungry dogs. Women's work. You're the one who wants to save the world. Men's work. Start by saving a puppy.'

'Yes, ma'am,' he said dazedly, still trying to come to terms with the sight of her peering anxiously into the darkness. Her backside-hugging jeans…cutest backside in the world! The smudge of dirt across her cheek as she rose to give him orders…

The whole damned package, in fact. The warmth, the care and the love in this place were threatening to overwhelm him.

But Rose wasn't overwhelmed in the least. 'Right now,' she said darkly, and stalked inside. 'T-Bone,' she added as she went, 'your master's home and he'll rescue your baby. Saving the world is all he's good for, so we might as well use him for that.'

He couldn't do it.

For the next half-hour Tom investigated every means known to man to get the puppy out. It simply wasn't possible without demolition. Access under the house was from the front, the house had sagged on its stumps some time over the last hundred years and there was about eight inches clearance between floor and ground.

He couldn't get through. Tom crawled in as far as he could, swearing all the time, calling to the puppy, spitting dust and finally retreating.

There was no way the puppy was leaving the light filtering through from the steps to come through the gloom towards him.

He gave it up as a bad job, then investigated the steps. They were built to last as long as the Great Pyramids— vast slabs of jarrah, eight feet long, three inches thick and two feet wide apiece.

The sides of the steps and the front of the verandah were built likewise, with gnarled trunks of ancient grapevines tangled through. To haul off a board would mean destroying the odd hundred-year-old grapevine.

Terrific!

The puppy whined on.

'Haven't you got him out yet?' Rose called sweetly from inside the house, and Tom ground his teeth.

Okay. There was only one thing to do here. He headed for the toolshed to find what he needed.

Rose emerged from feeding the twins, carrying one glass of lemonade and one mug of beer. She opened the screen door—and stared.

There was a hole in her verandah.

Stymied of any other access, Tom had resorted to ripping up the porch floorboards. He'd had to pull up half a dozen to get a gap big enough for him to get through. As each floorboard was twelve feet long, there was now a sizeable hole.

Rose stared down and her lips twitched.

'I was,' she said conversationally to the black hole in her porch, 'quite attached to my verandah.'

There was an oath from right underneath her—*right underneath her!*—and she jumped. The beer spilled, and then there was a sudden deathly silence and another oath—this one broader.

'What the hell...? Woman, what *are* you doing? *What are you pouring down on me?*'

Rose stared down in consternation, and then her lips twitched even more. Tom had shifted the boards at the side of the porch, rightly thinking that if he made the hole right at the door she might fall in. Then he'd climbed down his hole and crawled back along underneath so he was now right near the top of the steps—right underneath her. And when she'd spilled the beer the cracks and knot-holes in the ancient floorboards had been enough to let the beer go straight through.

'I—I thought you might like a beer instead of tea,' she said, trying hard to keep her voice deadpan.

'You thought I'd like it down my neck?'

'I didn't know where you were... where your neck was.'

'So you thought you'd just pour it on the off chance that my mouth was open ready to catch?'

'If you're as good at perilous situations as you say you are,' she said unsteadily, 'then I'd expect your reactions to be lightning-fast.'

There was an ominous silence at that, broken only by the pathetic whining of the puppy and the gurgling of two contented twins inside the house.

'How old did you say you were?' Tom demanded suddenly, weirdly, from under her.

'Twenty-seven. I had my birthday while you were away.'

That silenced him all over again. He sat back in the dust and it hit him hard. *She'd had her birthday while he was away.*

He hadn't even known.

'Why are you asking?' she asked pertly, and the sound

of her voice from right on top of him didn't help at all. It told him that she was standing right on top of his body, three inches away through the floorboards!

Somehow he had to get his voice working. Somehow he had to keep things light!

'Because it's a marvel that you've reached your twenty-seventh year without someone tarring and feathering you and running you out of town,' he managed. 'Rose, I can't get this dratted puppy to come to me. He's backing away into the step cavity.'

'Tell him you have beer,' she said, and he choked.

'Yeah, right. Here pup. Here pup, pup, pup. Nice pup. Come and taste some of Aunty Rose's beer.'

'You sound angry,' she said placidly.

'I don't sound angry.'

'You're sounding like you're trying not to sound angry. Babies can detect these sorts of things. They're amazingly sensitive.'

'Yeah, right…'

'You have to sound appealing. Sort of maternal.'

'You wouldn't like to come down and sound maternal yourself?' he said darkly, and she grinned.

'No way. I might get dirty.'

'Heaven forbid.'

'Hey, I know what you need!' She brightened, and down in the dark Tom flinched. There was cold, wet beer still trickling down his neck.

'No!'

'It'll work every time,' she said above him—and then there was a wuffle, a scrambling noise—and one vast maternal bloodhound launched itself down the hole into the darkness with him.

'Hey, not you, too,' Rose's voice called out in alarm, but it was too late. As Yoghurt—T-Bone—squirmed ecstatically through the dust towards Tom and her puppy, there was another scramble of paws and Boris went too, hauling himself down through the hole before Rose could catch him.

There was a yelp from under the house and it didn't come from a dog. It came from Tom—under dog! Under a lot of dog.

And then—

'No!' Rose yelled in alarm. 'Hey, stop!'

'No!' Tom yelled in accord—he was right with Rose on this one—but Rose's ability to keep six more squirming puppies away from a hole twelve feet long was hopeless.

One puppy landed down in the gloom, followed by two more.

'Good grief.' Rose sat back on her heels with three puppies wriggling in her arms—the three she'd managed to catch—and her lips twitched and twitched again. It was too much. She burst out laughing, and another puppy wriggled free and made it down the hole to its mother.

'Oh, Tom—Tom, I'm sorry.'

'You don't sound very sorry,' Tom said desperately. 'Rose, help me here.'

'You—'

'I'm drowning in dogs. I'm claustrophobic. It's a nightmare.'

Holy heck, his voice sounded *serious*! Rose's laughter eased a bit. Surely he wasn't serious about being claustrophobic? She lay down on her stomach and peered down the hole. A couple of tails and a few dopey ears, but otherwise all there was was darkness.

'Tom.'

'Rose, help!' His voice was choked with fear. What on earth...? Her concern growing, Rose leaned further under.

She was caught firmly under the arms, and hauled firmly down into the dusty cavity.

She squealed. *'No!'* But there was no gainsaying him.

He brooked no opposition, pulling her forward and under, so that before she realised what was happening she was lying with him in the dusty space between verandah floor and ground, with two great bloodhounds and seven ecstatic puppies wriggling adoringly around them.

'Ugh. Tom, no! Oh, you brute. Get away. Stop licking me.'

'I'm not licking you,' Tom said, affronted. 'What a thing to suggest!'

'I didn't mean—'

'Though come to think of it...'

'Tom, no!' A vast wet tongue hit her face and slurped, from chin to eyebrows, and she choked on laughter.

'That wasn't me,' Tom said firmly. 'I lick with more finesse than that. Want to feel?'

'No!'

'Rose, there's beer all over me,' he said soulfully. 'The dogs are licking me. All over. I don't know what you're complaining about. What's a little lick between friends?'

'You lied to me,' she managed through dog licks, shoving a great bloodhound head aside. 'You rat!'

'I didn't lie to you.' He was still holding her. They were lying full length in the dust and she could hardly see him, but she could feel him. She could feel his hands on her shoulders, his breath on her face. He was so close.

'You sounded—scared,' she managed. 'I thought something was wrong.

'I *was* scared,' he said with asperity. 'It's pretty scary to be buried under floorboards with a horde of wild dogs.'

'Wild dogs! Huh! Wild, my foot. Uncontrollable, however. A more disreputable, unruly bunch of— Okay, Boris, get off! I should have just put the floorboards back and locked you all down here for ever.'

'If that's what it takes to keep me here,' Tom said—and suddenly the whole thing changed.

Laughter died.

'What did you say?' Rose said at last.

'I guess…'

'Did you say—did you suggest you'd stay if I locked you up?'

'Rose…'

'Wait right here,' she said sternly, and put a finger on his nose. 'Don't you move.' And she hauled herself out of his arms, crept back through the dust and rose to peer out of the hole. Then she grabbed the boards and pulled them back, one after another, carefully slotting them into position. With the hole sealed so they were in almost total darkness except for the few slits of light coming from under the steps, she wriggled back to him.

'There,' she said breathlessly. 'Consider yourself locked in. My prisoner. My husband.'

She took his breath away. He wasn't ready for this. He wasn't sure what he was ready for. He was all at sea, and his rudder had fallen away a long time ago.

But he had no need of a rudder. No need of a sense of direction. Rose was in charge. She ignored the dogs weaving in and out around them. Her entire attention was focussed on him. Her hands came out and caught his face, holding him to her.

'Tom, I'm going nuts,' she said softly—softly but sternly. 'Since you left, I've been so unhappy, and I think—I can see it in your face—so have you.'

'No.'

'I love you so much,' she said gently. 'Are you telling me…are you able to look me in the eye and say truthfully that you're happy in that damned hotel room? Happier than here? With me? With your family?'

'No, but…'

'But what, Tom?'

'It'll hurt. When it ends.'

'Okay,' she said calmly. 'I've told you before. I'll accept that, and so can you. It'll hurt when—if—it has to end. But it hurts like crazy now. It can't get any worse. But you know what hurts the most now? It's knowing that you left when you didn't need to. Tom, I'm willing to accept any absences you need, as long as you *really need* them. Leave us when there's a world that needs saving or leave when you feel claustrophobic and you need an out—but don't go just because one of those events *might* happen in the fore-seeable future.'

'Rose.'

'Tom, take a chance,' she said, pleading. Her hands were on his face, her fingers warm. As if realising the seriousness of what was happening, the dogs had left off their bouncing. The pups were licking and were wuffling and snuffling with each other. Boris and T-Bone, though, were lying a dog apiece against man and woman, their big heads draped seriously over Rose's breast and Tom's thighs respectively. They looked as if they were listening for all they were worth—waiting for their fates.

Just like Rose.

'Tom, just go with the flow,' Rose said softly. 'Let yourself love us. We'll love you right back, but we won't hold you. I promise. Whenever you need to leave, we'll let you go—and whenever you come back we'll be here for you. Just—love us while you can.'

'Rose…' It was a groan, an aching tearing of his gut. She was so lovely. It was totally stupid to let himself get more immersed in this wonderful pool of loving—but how could he resist? How could any man?

'Stay, Tom,' she said softly, and she leaned forward and let her lips touch his—tasting, wanting, aching to have him hold her.

Aching for his love.

It was too much for any man, and it was too much for Tom. He groaned again, but this time the groan was different, and somewhere in Rose's chest a tiny bud of hope burst forth into flower. He couldn't resist. He couldn't!

'My love,' she whispered. 'My Tom...'

And then there was no need for more. He took her into his arms, gathered her to him in a fierce declaration of his submission—of his loving. The dogs didn't stand a chance of staying between them. Nothing could separate them now.

Boris and T-Bone didn't seem to mind. They rolled their eyes and then concentrated on each other. These people were boring.

And they were boring for a very, very long time.

Some time later these people surfaced to laughter, dust and a plethora of puppies. Bored in their dark kingdom, the pups had finally decided to investigate the passion-locked couple. No respecter of either persons or passion, they simply crawled all over them and started licking.

Laughing, Tom and Rose broke apart, disentangled themselves from each other and the pups, and emerged into daylight. Rose surfaced first and Tom handed up one dog after another. The pup that had been trapped had come out from under the steps long ago, joining his brothers and sisters in their tumbling.

'That makes seven pups, two dogs and two persons, all present and accounted for,' Rose said as Tom emerged. 'Quick, get the floorboards back and block the hole.'

'Yes, ma'am,' he said, and she chuckled.

'That's what I like. A nice subservient husband.' And she backed into the house before he could say a word.

By the time he had everything nailed down again, Rose had showered and changed. Tom walked into the house and was confronted with a glowingly clean wife. She was dressed in clean shorts and T-shirt, and she greeted her husband with disdain.

'Ugh! What a horror! Tom Bradley, you look disgusting.' She was cradling a twin, and now she lifted a gurgling Jessica to see. 'Jessica, take a look at this. Do you remember your daddy? No? I'm not surprised.' She grinned. 'He looks like something that crawled out from under the floorboards!'

Tom grinned back, but his attention was hardly on Rose any more. He walked the few steps forward so he could see Jessie.

Jess. His daughter. What had Rose said? 'Do you remember your daddy?' It was true. That was what she felt like. *His* daughter.

'Jessie.'

He smiled down at her, and as if in answer Jessica's tiny pink face creased into a round smile of delight. She looked up at him—and she grinned.

Tom's world dissolved right there on the spot. The hard casing around his heart, so carefully, painfully built up since his childhood, started disintegrating. Or maybe it didn't start then. Maybe it had started dissolving the first time he'd seen Rose, but now...now he could kid himself no longer. His defences were down and he was as exposed as he'd ever been. To love. To pain...

'Are they both...?'

'She's the only one smiling,' Rose told him, smiling herself as she watched his face. 'Toby's still serious. Jessica and I think it's because he's missing you.' Her smile died. 'So what do you say, Tom? Will you stay with us, or are you heading back to your hotel room? To your isolation?'

The world stilled, waiting for an answer. When he spoke, Tom knew what it had to be.

'I can't leave you,' he said simply. 'I can't bear to. I'll stay as long as I can.'

'Until there's a fire to fight?'

'It's what I do, Rose,' he said helplessly. He hadn't travelled any further than that in his thoughts. He was still a hell-fighter.

'Mmm.'

He looked at her face and could see thoughts crowded in—thoughts that he had no way of facing. Thoughts like, Why don't you farm? This farm could be so productive. Why don't you change what you do?

But Rose didn't voice her thoughts. How could she? She was fighting with everything she had, for as much as he was prepared to give. He'd just learned to give his love. The fact that she wanted his life to change could wait, and if it didn't—well, she'd love him on any terms he cared to name.

'That's fine by us, Tom,' she said gently. 'Just stay. Until the world needs you, accept that we need you more. Love us, and let us love you in return.'

That night, lying with Rose nestled in his arms, with the warmth of her naked body making him feel as he'd never felt in his life before, Tom even felt himself wishing for a long, long time before the next fire.

So why couldn't he become a farmer?

No way. He had to go. He must! He was geared to fighting fires. It was his life. To switch off, to become a husband and a farmer and father scared him stupid—but he'd have this time...

And if the next fire was a long time coming, so be it. For now, he was content.

CHAPTER TEN

THE next fire arrived in ten days.

Rose was in town taking the twins for a health check. If she hadn't been away, she might have answered Tom's phone, Charlie might have learned of her existence and who knew what might have happened? As it was, Tom was home alone and he lifted the phone at the first ring.

'You still waiting in that damned hotel for a call?'

'What's wrong, Charlie?' Straight away, Tom heard the tension in Charlie's voice—an edge that meant that every part of his brain was concentrating solely on the job at hand, and he knew straight off that it had to be a big one.

'Steve's in trouble. There's three wells down there and one's been burning for two weeks. We don't know how the hell it started, and just as it was getting under control it blew again and another one started up. We're looking at sabotage.'

'Yeah?' Tom grimaced. This was the sort of burn the team hated. It was hard enough battling wildfire without having to watch your back, knowing there were people around who were willing you to fail and probably prepared to go to extraordinary lengths to see that you did.

Most times all the teams had to worry about were rattle-snakes—plus the fires. To have saboteurs as well...

They had them there, and Charlie's worry was etched in his voice.

'There's been a couple of security guards shot,' Charlie said tersely. 'It's a bloody mess, Tom. Steve's up to his eyeballs with the first fire, he can't go anywhere now without bodyguards, everyone knows him and he's a target—

166

so he's called for back-up. It's slowing him down, and it's too big for one operator. Joanne's said she'll go, but she's still hotheaded. If you want to—'

'Joanne…'

'She's a fine firefighter and she wants her day in the sun, but I'm not dead sure she's ready. If you're still champing at the bit, I'll put her second in charge behind you. Give her a bit more training in sticky situations. She's only done straight fires until now.' He hesitated. 'Though you know you don't have to go, Tom. You've done your bit. I like retiring my best from the front line before they push their luck too far. But you said you wanted—'

'Yeah.'

Charlie's keen ears pricked at that. 'You having doubts, boy?'

Tom stared slowly around the room. Doubts? Yes, he was having doubts. Scores of them. There were baby toys and puppies from one end of the kitchen to the other. Outside, he could see Sam coupling the plough to the tractor. Tom had intended to spend the day ploughing the south paddock, and the thought of spending hours tilling neat rows, with nine dogs tearing along in the furrows beside him—with the prospect of coming in after a long day's work to find Rose and the babies waiting for him—had given him real pleasure.

But the thought of letting others take—what had Charlie said?—his place in the sun, his last piece of independence, the last armour-plate around his heart…

No. He couldn't bear it.

I'll do it this time, he told himself. One more piece of action.

One more time of being…*me*.

'Of course you have to go.' Rose's reaction was swift, and if Tom hadn't seen the sudden draining of colour from her face he might have thought she didn't care. But he had. She did.

'It might be a month,' he said slowly, watching her face. 'Before I come back.'

'But...' her heart was in her eyes now, and her pain was there for all to see '...you will come back? Promise me.'

He moved then, crossing swiftly to take her into his arms, against his heart. 'I'll come back.'

'The work you do...' Her voice fell away to a whisper.

He cupped her chin so he could meet her eyes. 'The work I do?'

'I was going to ask if it was dangerous,' she managed. 'But Marty died. So don't tell me.'

'I'm very good at what I do,' he told her.

'And Marty wasn't?'

Silence. There was no sound, just the feel of her heart, pounding against his. He could feel her fear.

Maybe...

No. He *had* to do this. *It was what he did!*

It was the last part of his aloneness, his last barrier from the pain of total commitment.

'I need to go, Rose,' he said softly, kissing her hair.

'Why? Because Charlie needs you to go—or because *you* need you to go?'

There was no way he could answer that question. They both knew the truth without him having to voice it.

'Toby hasn't smiled yet,' she said bleakly. 'You'll miss it.'

'Take a picture?'

'Sure.' She choked back the beginning of a sob and managed a smile, albeit a watery one. 'Of course. I'll take heaps. You come back next month and I'll have every move documented.'

'And you won't sell the pups while I'm away?'

'They're nearly two months old now,' she objected. 'They're ready to go at eight weeks, and they're eating me out of house and home.'

'I need to vet their new owners,' Tom growled, hiding his emotion by bending down and scooping up a waddling pup. The pup did a long-tongued lick—their parents were training them well—and the slurpy affection made Tom feel worse. 'I want the right homes for each of them.'

'As long as you're back in four weeks.'

'I will be,' he promised. He must… To stay away longer was unthinkable.

'Okay, then. Go,' Rose said, and lifted the puppy from his arms. 'Just go, Tom Bradley. And get back to your family fast!'

'We're laying water pipes now. Come Saturday there'll be enough water pressure for you to start. Joanne's already out there, organising bulldozers to clear the mess around the well as soon as we cool it down.'

'Any trouble with equipment?' Tom's voice was steady, but Charlie eyed him sideways. Something was different and he didn't know what.

'No. We're putting everything we can into this one. Lucky it's in Mexico. The last one out in Sumatra was a real headache trying to get the stuff we needed. I got the Christmas trees—three sets on site already. We're doubling up all round in case the looney who struck once strikes again. Steve used one tree to put out the south well but someone shoved it full of plastic explosive. Whoom! Had to start all over. The lad's less than pleased.'

'I imagine he might be,' Tom said dryly. 'He got the tree closed okay?' The 'Christmas trees' were sets of valves shoved down over the well pipes after the fire had been doused, and gradually closed to form a seal.

'Yeah, but no longer. Now he's waiting for repairs to his

water supply to start again. By the look of it, you might get your well out first.'

'I'll do my best.'

'Watch your back,' Charlie said warningly. 'There's something going on here I don't like. Political stuff, maybe.'

'I'll be careful.'

But Charlie was still watching his face. 'There's nothing I ought to know?' he said slowly. 'You look…different.'

'I had a holiday.'

'Nothing's changed?'

'Nothing's changed.' Ha! But he couldn't tell Charlie. Not now.

'Well, as I said,' Charlie said uncomfortably. 'watch your back. And let Joanne help.'

'You've come a long way,' Tom teased. 'Letting women on the team.'

'There's a place for them everywhere,' Charlie said simply, 'and I think I know that better than you do, boy.'

'Yeah, right…'

'This Rose you talked about—'

'I'm leaving, Charlie,' Tom said hurriedly. 'See you when we debrief. For now, I've a plane to catch.'

When he left, Charlie stood looking after him for a long time. He knew his men, did Charlie, and he didn't like not knowing.

The sensation of unease stayed with him over the next few days as he listened to reports of the Mexico fires from his base in Houston. The north fire Tom was fighting was a ripper—flames shooting four hundred feet in the air. The ecological damage was causing government officials, and even the world health organisations, to have apoplexies.

It seemed straightforward enough. Tom's plan was to produce enough water pressure to cool things so he could clear the well surrounds. The water pressure on its own wouldn't be enough to douse the powerful flame. He'd have to lay plastic explosives, using the ensuing blast to suck the oxygen from the air so the flame would die. Then, under cover of the water, he'd have to get in fast to set the Christmas tree.

It was filthy, dangerous work, and it was as tricky an operation as Charlie had ever been involved in. This fire was vast and he didn't like it one bit. Not because he didn't think Tom could cope—if anyone could, Tom could. Sure, the fire was huge, but that wasn't the major problem. Mostly he worried because the saboteurs were still unaccounted for.

There was an element of the unknown here, and Charlie hated unknowns.

And it was the same with Tom...

'He's changed,' he told his wife a few days later, on the eve of the day Tom planned to set off his explosives and kill the flame. 'I don't know maybe... Maybe... He told me he'd met a woman but he was joking.'

'A woman? Our Tom?' Maddie said with pleasure. 'It's about time.'

'I told you,' Charlie said irritably. 'He was joking. He even said he was married. With twins...'

'It's an odd sort of joke, dear,' Maddie said slowly. 'Are you sure he wasn't serious?'

'Oh, yeah. Married and twins in six weeks...'

'So what's he got on his Red Alert?' Maddie said. The Red Alerts were the forms kept at head office giving every single detail of each team member's life, including next of kin. After one of his men had died before he could contact his family, Charlie had insisted that the last thing every member did before they left on a burn was update the Red Alert.

'I'll look tomorrow.'

'You do that, dear,' Maddie said serenely. 'And stop worrying. Tom can look after himself.'

'Holy heck.'

Charlie stood by his desk and stared down at the form in blank amazement.

Yeah, it was updated.

In the space marked 'Next of kin', the word 'Mother' had been neatly crossed out. Instead, there was a new word.

'Wife'.

'Wife, Rose Marie Bradley.'

And under that there was attached an envelope marked 'Last will and testament', a document so new the ink had barely dried on the front of the envelope.

It was none of his business, but there were some times a man just had to pry, and this was certainly one of them. Charlie ripped open the envelope and stared down in amazement.

A legal will, leaving his possessions 'to my beloved wife…and to my two children, Jessica Margaret and Tobias Thomas…'

Holy heck.

'He's married! He has kids!' Charlie said explosively. 'And I've sent him off in charge! Doesn't he know company policy? Ten years. Ten years and then you're out of the firing line unless you have no dependants. Let someone else take the risks. What does he think he's playing at?'

He put his hand on the telephone, but as he did it started to ring.

It had all been going like clockwork. No job was totally without complications but this one—sure, it was a big fire, but the team Tom was leading knew their job like the back of their hands and Joanne was second-guessing his orders.

Every time he turned to give an order he found it ready to
be carried out. Charlie ran a tight ship and Tom had never
appreciated it as much as he did now. He could leave and
the machinery would keep on whirring without him.

And, as he waited for the last explosion, he knew he
would leave. This suddenly seemed like work. Despite the
risk it had never seemed like that before.

Before he'd met Rose it had kept him going—the adren-
alin, the knife-edge risk of playing with such vast forces,
the filth, the dangers of the fire itself and the poisonous
fumes containing sulphur dioxide, arsenic, lead, copper—
and the heat... It had all filled an emptiness in him that
ached to be filled.

And now that need was no longer there. Something had
changed in him. There was no longer this aching restlessness.

Or maybe there was. Maybe he'd learned something, he
thought as he stared out over the parched, scorched land-
scape to the tower of flames beyond. Maybe the restlessness
now was to go home.

Home.

He'd thought he still needed this, but now he knew he
didn't. This was the last job. He'd really made that decision
as he'd gone in himself under cover of the vast jets of water
to lay the dynamite charges. His mind was no longer here.
It was busy making plans. Maybe he'd stay on as a con-
sultant, but he wouldn't attend fires any more. He'd use
some of his savings and buy up the farm next door to
Rose's. It was practically derelict. He'd build it up, and
turn their combined farm into the biggest, best, most beautiful in the district. He'd make a life for his family...

'Ready, boss?'

'Yeah.' Tom glanced at his watch. Two minutes to blast
time. The cranes were in position. The vast pumps were
aimed to spread tons of water in minutes. Once the first

blast occurred they'd wait only long enough to see if the flame was out before the water hit the seat of the fire, cooling it enough for the 'tree' to be positioned.

'Go!'

Tom didn't need the shout from his foreman. It was followed by a boom so big the earth trembled under his feet.

'It's worked!' Joanne was first out of their bunker, shading her eyes and practically bristling with excitement. Forty years old, weathered, agile, mother of two grown sons, Joanne was aching to prove herself in this world of danger. 'It's out. I'm moving!'

'Wait, Jo—' Tom yelled warningly. He wanted time. Not normally—normally the team moved like streaked lightning as soon as the lack of oxygen caused by the blast made the fire die. But there was the unknown...

It was too late. Joanne had reached the first Jeep and was swinging herself aboard, shoving her mask over her face. 'What's keeping you?' she yelled.

But Tom was no longer watching her. There was a sixth sense at work here. This had been too easy.

He swung his glasses slowly around, checking out the horizon. His team had cleared every last inch of this land, setting up barricades for miles. But...

On the top of the next ridge he saw the sudden glint of field glasses...

'No, wait,' he shouted, and was out of there like a flash, yelling into his radio. 'Jo— Blast, what's her frequency? Hell, she hasn't left it on.'

And then, because there was no other way and he suddenly knew—without sense or reason but he knew!—exactly what would happen he dropped everything and ran.

'Stay!' he roared at the foreman. 'No one move from the bunkers. Except Security. Get them back to the south ridge.

There's someone up there watching. But everyone else—
no one move anywhere!'

He reached the second Jeep and took off after Joanne as
if the fires of hell were after him.

He nearly made it back.

Nearly, but not quite.

'Mrs Bradley?'

The voice was that of an older man and it was tight with
tension. Rose knew it was disaster at once. It had to be.
How many people rang at three in the morning to talk about
the weather? Her feet turned to ice on the stone-flagged
floor, and she leaned against the wall for support.

She knew.

'Tom? Oh, God, Tom?'

'He's alive,' the voice said, and only Charlie knew what
an effort it cost him not to break down as he said the word.

That was something. Rose's world steadied a smidgen.
Alive. But—'Hurt?'

'Yes.'

'H—how?'

'Saboteurs,' Charlie said grimly. 'Trying to destroy the
team. They knew that we blast the seat of the fire to put
out the flame and we stay in bunkers while we do it. They
couldn't get near the bunkers and they couldn't get near
the fire—we had the place guarded. But they knew the team
would be moving fast after the blast and they'd be moving
in a tight-packed convoy. We have time for nothing else.
So they set explosives between the well and the bunker. As
soon as the flame died, when they thought we'd all be moving, they set them to explode.'

'But—but Tom…' Rose's heart was a frozen lump. 'He
was… Oh, dear God, no.'

'It's not as bad as it sounds,' Charlie said hurriedly, hop-
ing to hell it was the truth. 'There were only the two hurt.

One of the team members was a bit anxious, left early, and your Tom sensed something was up. Took off after her. Got her almost back to the bunker before the blast. Joanne escaped with bruises. Tom, though…'

'Tell me,' she said, and her voice was suddenly calm. He wasn't dead, she thought blankly. Anything was better than that. Anything was possible, given that.

'He was hit by flying debris,' Charlie said heavily. 'He has a compressed skull fracture. He's unconscious. I'm sorry, ma'am, but that's all I can tell you. The doctors don't know more.'

'Where—? Oh, God, I'll come.' Her knees had gone on her completely. Rose slumped down onto the floor, cradling the receiver like a lifeline. 'Where is he?'

'You tell me where you are,' Charlie growled. 'I'll have a car pick you up within the hour. There's a private jet lined up at Sydney. We'll bring you straight to him—'

'The twins,' Rose said, trying to sort out some sort of sense from her panic. Now wasn't the time for hysteria. 'I'll come…of course I'll come, but I'll have to bring the twins.'

'He really has twins?'

'I— He really has twins.'

'How old?'

'Two months.'

'Well, I'll be…' Charlie paused, taking this on board. 'Bring them too,' he said heavily. 'I'll make arrangements. Seems to me our Tom needs all the family he can get.'

CHAPTER ELEVEN

'JOAN?'

'Yes, dear?' It might be three in the morning, but Joan Mitchell knew trouble when she heard it.

'I'm leaving for Mexico. Will you take care of the dogs? Sam's away for the night. Tell him when he comes back...'

'My dear.' Joan was out of bed and poking her recumbent husband. 'Bob, wake up. Our Rose is in trouble.'

Our Rose... How different it all was now, Rose thought fleetingly. Thanks to Tom.

'It's Tom?'

'He's hurt—' Rose's voice broke on a sob. 'Joan, I have to go.'

'Of course you do. And the twins?'

'They're coming with me,' Rose said fiercely. 'He needs all his family. But—I can't take the dogs. And he needs us all.'

'Mrs Bradley?' The vast dark limousine had slipped so silently into the yard that Rose hadn't heard it. Now she stared out into the darkened front porch to see a uniformed chauffeur courteously waiting.

'Yes.' She was so at sea she couldn't think straight. She'd dressed and thrown a few things into a suitcase but she didn't have a clue what to pack—what she'd need.

But the man was smiling, his expression so paternal she could almost feel a pat on the head. 'I'm here to help,' he said. 'The nanny service in the US sent me through a list of baby requirements on the car fax. Mr. Patterson thought

177

you'd very likely be too rushed to make your own list so he's provided one for you. Let's just go through it and make sure we have everything we need for the flight.'

'Yes.'

'And if we don't, don't worry. There's a trained mothercraft nurse meeting us at the airport for the flight. We'll fax her now and she'll supply everything we don't have. Now, let's get these babies packed.' He paused as the first of seven puppies bounced towards him. 'These…'

'They're not coming,' Rose said bleakly. 'Oh, but I wish they were.'

'I have orders,' the chauffeur said. 'We might not be able to take them, but let's see what else we can do with them.'

'Rose?'

Rose paused at the top of the steps of the private jet, shading her eyes against the harsh Mexican sun. She was exhausted. She'd been treated like royalty but she'd flown half way around the world and she'd stared straight ahead every inch of the way. There was a prayer in her head and she dared not stop uttering it for a moment. 'Please. Please…'

Somewhere in the aircraft there were two mothercraft nurses—the Australian nurse had been left in Los Angeles to fly home, and two American girls had come with her on the smaller plane down to Mexico. They'd brought her the twins to feed, and to cuddle when they thought she needed it, but otherwise she'd been left alone with her prayers.

Now she stood on the top step and watched as a grizzly bear of a man lunged up the steps to take her hand.

'Mrs Bradley. Rose. I'm Charlie Patterson. Tom's boss. There's been no change.'

Rose let her breath out in a rush. She'd known. She'd been so sure she'd be able to feel it if—if he'd died, but to hear he was definitely alive was a comfort.

'What do the doctors say?' she asked calmly, but she leaned on Charlie heavily as she came down the steps.

'There's been some intracranial bleeding,' he said, 'but we don't know much more than that. I've flown in the best specialists money can buy, and all they can say is that we have to wait and see. They operated to relieve the pressure. They've done everything they can.'

'I'm sure.'

'This is my wife, Maddie.'

An older lady was waiting at the foot of the steps. She came forward now and took Rose into her arms, hugging hard.

'Oh, my dear. I had to come with Charlie. Our Tom... That we had to meet like this. And he didn't tell us... He has twins!'

'I— They're not his,' Rose said bleakly. 'I was a widow when we met.'

'I see.' Maddie's face cleared. This made sense. But... 'You're wrong, dear,' she said gently. 'I know it's prying, but before he left for Mexico Tom left a will. Charlie showed it to me, and he's made it clear. "My beloved wife", he calls you. And "my children". Jessica and Tobias. *My* children.'

'Oh, God,' Rose said, and burst into tears.

That was the last time she cried for three days. The initial shock and emotion over, she switched into organisation drive and the tiny hospital Tom was in had never seen anything like it. Charlie had offered to fly him to America's finest hospitals but 'We want that head immobile', the surgeon had growled, and he'd been stymied. He'd had to content himself with flying in enough staff and equipment to keep his memory green in the district for years.

'You save him and it's yours to keep,' Charlie told the

hospital administrator. 'Plus a donation to make your head spin. See what you can do for this patient.'

But there was nothing he could do in the end. Despite all the equipment and care that money could buy, there was nothing for it but to wait. And hope.

But Rose used the waiting time. Thanks to Charlie's efficient chauffeur, she'd brought so much she could use! She was never more than a few feet from Tom's bedside, sleeping in a makeshift bed close by, and when she was awake she was active.

Please, God, if only it worked.

'Tom…'

Three days. Three interminable days!

There was nothing more she could do. She sat and held his hand, willing warmth and strength into the limp fingers. He was so still, so pale. Her Tom.

'Tom, please… God, please…'

She waited. And waited.

Tom opened his eyes to dogs.

He was surrounded by dogs, dogs and more dogs, interspersed with babies. He'd never seen so many dogs in all his life.

He blinked, the light hurt and he closed his eyes again fast. Dogs and babies—he was obviously in some sort of dream.

But he wasn't, and Rose had seen that blink.

She'd been sitting, patiently watching, just as she'd watched for three long days. As she'd watch for three months if she must, or three long years. Now she leaned forward and gripped his hand, twining her fingers in his. Surely she'd seen—surely she hadn't imagined it?

'Tom?'

And the tiny flicker of movement in his face told her she hadn't been wrong.

'Tom!'

As he opened his eyes again, she buried her face in his chest and closed her own eyes. Her prayer changed. Even if he woke, there was a possibility of brain damage, they'd said. So… 'Please…'

'Why?' Tom said carefully in a voice that creaked with disuse. 'Why am I surrounded by dogs?'

Her eyes flew wide open and her head snapped up. Tom was staring around the room as if he was going nuts. And in her heart a tiny bubble of joy burst forth and exploded outwards like a thousand shards of light.

'They're your puppies,' she said. 'Your babies. Don't you recognise them?'

'My…'

She pointed to the walls, where poster-sized photographs of puppies gazed down from every conceivable angle, with the odd baby photograph interspersed—and her eyes misted with love. 'While you were away we named them.'

'We…?'

'Jess and Toby and I. We figured you'd never let us sell them so we might as well roll with the punches. That one's Ferdinand. There's Lester and Gerty and Clyde and Billy. And Sophie's the one with the hugest eyes and Fatso's the one who fell through the step.'

'Fatso,' he said faintly.

'I know it's not nice,' she said, and turned to take his hand again, her eyes devouring him. Pinching herself to make sure she wasn't dreaming. 'But we ran out of inspiration.'

'Charlie,' he said strongly. 'After someone I know…'

And that did it. Brain damage, my foot. Ha! She lifted his hand in hers, put his fingers against her cheek and burst into tears.

'He wants to see his daddy.' Maddie peered round the door, her arms full of baby, and when she saw Tom's eyes move towards her her face creased in pleasure. 'Oh, my dear. They told me you were awake and okay.' She bustled forward to the bed, and Rose moved aside—just—so Maddie could kiss him. 'Oh, my dear...'

'The twins are here?' Tom said with pleasure, though his voice weakened with the effort. 'I thought they were just more photos on my walls.'

'Wasn't it clever of Charlie's man to take all those photographs while Rose packed?' Maddie said. 'Charlie told him to bring everything that was needed to make you feel at home, and he couldn't bring your dogs so he did the next best thing.'

'Very clever.'

'Now, I'm not to stay,' Maddie beamed. 'The doctor says two minutes. But I knew you'd want to see Toby.' She pulled down the shawl and Toby's bright little eyes peered out at the world. 'Isn't he just the darlingest thing? But I still can't make him smile. He's almost nine weeks old and Rose says he hasn't grinned once.'

The baby was six inches from Tom's nose. Tom looked into those wonderful little eyes—Rose's eyes—and Toby stared back, a picture of intense concentration.

'Tobias Thomas Bradley,' Tom said faintly, and took a tiny fist between his fingers. Solemnly he shook hands—and he smiled.

And Toby smiled right back.

It was the party to end all parties.

The world's biggest marquee was up on the home paddock. There were hay bales stretched as far as the eye could see, grouped as seats and tables for the mass of wondrous food—as well as forming a stage for the best fiddle-player the country boasted, with a back-up band of musicians whose talents were only matched by their enjoyment of the occasion.

There were balloons and streamers and lights. There were fireworks shooting skywards into the brilliant, starlit autumn night.

And people—there were people everywhere, dancing, laughing, singing—passing babies from hand to hand, patting the dogs…

Because, of course, there were dogs—huge velvety dogs that moved from person to person, asking for adoration. There weren't many homes in the world that could accommodate nine full-grown bloodhounds without a blink, but… 'How could we choose which ones to sell and how can we part with any?' Tom had demanded, and Rose had grinned.

'Yeah, you take your attitude into cattle-rearing, Farmer Bradley, and we're in big trouble.'

'Yes, ma'am.'

The discussion had ended in laughter.

Laughter… There'd been a constant ripple of laughter in this home for the last twelve months. Laughter and joy and dogs and babies—and so much happiness it radiated out through the district.

And further—world-wide. Charlie and Maddie and Joanne and Steve and all the team were here tonight. There'd better not be a well-fire anywhere in the world, because the hell-fighters were busy—otherwise engaged on very important business.

They were attending the christening of one Madeleine Rose Bradley, two weeks old, sister to Jessie and Toby.

She'd been delivered at home after a labour that lasted

all of twenty minutes. It was just as well the father was experienced.

'She's our tenth baby,' Rose said softly as she stood at Tom's side, her newest daughter in her arms. 'Oh, Tom, how can life possibly get any better than this?'

'Just watch this space,' Tom said gently, a twin in each arm and surrounded by adoring dogs. 'Watch this space, my love. Because it will.'

MILLS & BOON®

Makes any time special™

Mills & Boon publish 29 new titles every month. Select from...

Modern Romance™   Tender Romance™

Sensual Romance™

Medical Romance™   Historical Romance™

MAT2

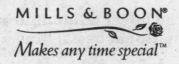

The latest triumph from
international bestselling author

Debbie Macomber

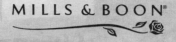

brings you

PROMISE

*Share the lives—and loves—of the
people in Promise, Texas.
A town with an interesting past
and an exciting future.*

Available from 21st July

0008/114/MB5a

books and a surprise gift!

We would like to take this opportunity to thank you for reading this Mills & Boon® book by offering you the chance to take TWO more specially selected titles from the Tender Romance™ series absolutely FREE! We're also making this offer to introduce you to the benefits of the Reader Service™—

- ★ FREE home delivery
- ★ FREE gifts and competitions
- ★ FREE monthly Newsletter
- ★ Exclusive Reader Service discounts
- ★ Books available before they're in the shops

Accepting these FREE books and gift places you under no obligation to buy, you may cancel at any time, even after receiving your free shipment. Simply complete your details below and return the entire page to the address below. *You don't even need a stamp!*

YES! Please send me 2 free Tender Romance books and a surprise gift. I understand that unless you hear from me, I will receive 4 superb new titles every month for just £2.40 each, postage and packing free. I am under no obligation to purchase any books and may cancel my subscription at any time. The free books and gift will be mine to keep in any case.

N0ZEA

Ms/Mrs/Miss/Mr ....Initials...............................
                                                        BLOCK CAPITALS PLEASE

Surname ....

Address ....

....

....Postcode.................

Send this whole page to:
UK: FREEPOST CN81, Croydon, CR9 3WZ
EIRE: PO Box 4546, Kilcock, County Kildare (stamp required)